Crave

Crave

DARNELLA FORD

 St. Martin's Griffin ❧ New York

www.stmartins.com

Library of Congress Cataloging-in-Publication Data

Ford, Darnella.
    Crave / Darnella Ford.—1st ed.
        p.   cm.
    ISBN 0-312-30407-2
    1. African American women—Fiction.   2. Mate selection—Fiction.
 Single women—Fiction.   I. Title.

 606.O73C73 2004
    6—dc22

                                                    2003058776

      6   5   4   3

To those who died in the fire because they danced with the flame. To those who perished in the desert because the rain never came. To those who evaporated into nothingness because the sun got down on its knees. And to those who took the bullet in the chest because they managed to believe that not only did love exist, but that *somehow* they might actually find it in their lifetime. I wrote this book for *you*.

ACKNOWLEDGMENTS

I am so grateful for another opportunity to do this once mo' again. I am grateful to the people who continue to make this dream a reality for me. To my editor, Monique Patterson, I thank you for taking me to the next level. I am convinced that you deposit just as much of your *soul* into my novels as I do. And to St. Martin's Press, *thank you* for continuing to believe and take chances on this "simple chick" who often wanted to "write life" even more than she wanted to live it. To my agent, Claudia Menza, I continue to be in awe of your integrity *and* your compassion.

To the book clubs, booksellers, and readers who supported me with *Rising*, I thank you! Thank you! Thank you! A special thanks to the many readers who took a moment to drop me an e-mail. I have cherished your every word.

To "the one" who stole my heart back in 1997—my little girl, Morgan. You are the reason I get out of bed each day and try. I love you more than one lifetime will allow me. You are the sole reason I continue to believe I still have enough wind in my sails to float and just enough air in my belly to *fly*.

Have you?

Have you ever?

Have you ever craved someone?

Have you ever craved someone so bad?

Have you ever craved someone so bad you could feel?

Have you ever craved someone so bad you could feel your heart?

Have you ever craved someone so bad you could feel your heartbeat
  still?

Beat still

Beat still

Beat

And they—

Didn't crave you back?

Crave

1

GENESIS

There are countless numbers of people who walk around each day with a gaping hole in the middle of their heart and as a result they leak.

And long.

Need.

Ache.

And *crave*.

On one hand they are convinced love no longer exists, but on the other hand, they have devoted their entire lives to finding it. They become their relationships and their relationships become them as they take up the pursuit of a soul mate as a full-time occupation. These are the very people who walk, jog, run, and sprint aimlessly in whatever direction love was last seen in. Their every relationship is staggering and earth shattering.

Every one is *the one*.

Every disappointment is a devastation.

Every day is greeted by yet another opportunity to fall for the least unavailable human being on the planet. Every heartbreak tacks another six months in therapy onto time already served. They are so desperate for love they become stalkers of their own vision, seekers of their own illusion. And perhaps this is the most tragic element of all.

They will hunt it down.

Rope it.

Chain it.

Capture and inevitably kill love before realizing that the thing they search for is intangible and evasive. It is also aloof and fragile. These are also the same people who will spend their entire lives searching for love before realizing it does not make itself available to be found. They will extend themselves beyond heaven and earth to catch a glimpse of it before coming into the devastating knowledge that it is indeed invisible.

These are the people who entered the world hungry and needy, crowning headfirst from their mother's vagina with both eyes open, supercharged in their quest for love. They have transcended worlds, generations of time, and shape-shifted through many souls to find that which makes them whole and human. And of *these* people, I am the foremost.

Hold on.

Foreplay please.

I must officially introduce myself.

My name is Michael.

Hold up.

I am a girl.

I know the name rings of masculinity, but the day I was born these were the conditions: my father wanted a boy and my mother was on morphine. And that's how I came to be Michael Morgan for life.

My parents were seminormal, I think.

Hold on.

Rewind.

My parents may have been anything (read between the lines "everything") but normal. Don't take my word on it, though. You will come to your own understanding of their idiosyncrasies in due time and this much I promise you.

Please allow me to introduce my mother, Colleen. Sometimes I refer to her as the Mama Bear, probably a direct result of my childhood obsession with *Goldilocks and the Three Bears*.

Mama Bear had beautiful brown skin.

Hips to the east and west of her small waist.

Plump breasts and big hair.

The moment I was expelled from her uterus and went "air born," she started tripping, and this was my genesis. The early days included random lullabies by the Mama Bear, which foreshadowed clues of her emotional instability.

Hush little baby don't you cry,
'Cause I jump out of my skin first and then I'll die.
Hush little baby don't shed a tear,
'Cause the Mother Goose will run away from here.

What version of "Hush Little Baby" was that, Mama Bear?

Damn.

"Isn't she perfect?" declared Mama Bear one night while

pausing from her illogical nursery rhyme just long enough to consult with her husband, Sergio. Sergio was my father, but naturally, I often referred to him as the Papa Bear.

Papa Bear was the son of a Cuban immigrant and a black ditch digger. He was a beautiful mix of two struggling cultures, but I always felt that his greatest struggles were those found within the iron chains of matrimony, because Mama Bear was no picnic. No picnic at all.

Papa Bear bled into the background and was often upstaged by his wife's theatrics. He had two full-time jobs: street sweeper by day, punching bag for the Mama Bear by night.

"Isn't she perfect, Sergio?" snapped Mama Bear again because the Papa Bear did not answer her right away. "I didn't hear you say how absolutely perfect she was today. Aren't you listening? You're not listening to me are you, Sergio?" she asked, beginning to pout.

No one listens.

No one cares.

No one listens.

And no one cares.

Pouting was the norm for Mama Bear. As a matter of fact, I can hardly remember a time when Mama Bear wasn't pouting and pulling at Papa Bear's sideburns for all of his attention. Mama Bear didn't work outside the home, but she did work the last nerve of everyone in it. Tiresome and laborious were her daily mantras.

Sergio!

Sergio!

I need you to do this.

And do that.

I need you to be this and to be that.

Can you fetch, sit up, bark, and roll over?

Can you jump over the moon?

Chase after the sun?

"Sergio!" she snapped. "I cannot believe you're just standing there like a deaf-mute! Aren't you going to acknowledge how perfect your daughter is?"

"She's beautiful, dear," he would say just to appease my mother. Not that he didn't think I was beautiful, but was probably sick to death of his wife reminding him of it every second of every day for the last five and a half years.

"Perfect!" she would counter with a hiss. "I didn't ask you if she was beautiful, I asked you if she was perfect!" Papa Bear would pretend to ignore her, and she would be reduced to yet another dramatic performance.

"You don't love me anymore, do you?" wailed the tiresome Mama Bear. "And my twenty-eight hours of labor to deliver this child was in vain. And this nasty C-section scar on my bikini line was all for nothing," she pouted. "Sliced like a pig at the slaughter and it means *nothing* to you!" she bellowed, grinding on her husband's patience.

"Come on, Mother," said Papa Bear extending a stern voice and a free hand to his wife's tense shoulders. "Calm yourself down," he said coaxing his size eleven shoe between the truth and her attitude.

"I went through hell so I could have your child!"

"Will you let the child be?" Papa Bear said. "Come on, Colleen, and let her sleep."

"I love to watch her sleep," said Mama Bear with a great sigh. "She is perfect, isn't she Sergio? Just perfect."

"Come on, Mother," said Papa Bear, pulling on her pajama sleeves.

They would eventually leave my room and let me be, but Mama Bear would never let me be for long. How could she allow anything to be when she was so desperate to find her own blend of human perfection right here on earth?

I was six when I discovered how critical perfection was to Mama Bear. It was the day my mother decided to teach me to ride that evil demon known as the bicycle. The day would have been a blur if I didn't have such a sharp memory for details and devastation.

"It's time for you to learn how to ride a bike," she said one hot, muggy summer day, walking me to an abandoned field near the railroad tracks by our house. Dressed in all white, she yanked me down the road by one hand and the bike by the other. I stared at the bike with big eyes, taking it all in. It was so much bigger than me—to the point of being a monstrosity.

"Mama Bear," I said, because that's what I always called her. "How do you ride a bike?"

"I'll show you, angel," she snapped impatiently.

Mama Bear looked frantic and nervous, which at the time didn't alarm me because that was her typical look. By the time we found the "perfect spot," the Mama Bear had begun to sweat and her hair was unraveling from the inside out.

"Okay, angel," she said, pointing to the bike. "Pay attention. You're going to get on this bike, and I'm going to push you. Then I'm going to let go, and you're going to pedal fast and ride off into the sunset and catch the moon."

"Where am I going?" I asked again for clarification. *Off into the sunset to catch the moon* seemed like bogus directions to a six-year-old.

"Off into the sunset!" she shouted. "Like the old movie stars in the classics . . ."

I nodded.

What the hell?

"Everything has a happy ending in the movies," insisted Mama Bear. "Now get on that bike and ride off into the sunset."

Come on Mama Bear, even slow kids know that not everything has a happy ending.

"Come on, angel," demanded Mother, impatiently tapping her foot.

I cautiously mounted the bike as Mother held it steady. *What the hell happened to the training wheels?* And then without warning and like a raging bat out of hell she sped down the dirt road like a Lear jet, laughing wildly with her hair blowing in the wind. Her white flared pants looked like giant sails on top of ocean waters.

"Pedal! Pedal!" she cackled and hollered. "Ride off into the sunset!" was all I remembered her saying before she let go of the bike and I rode off into the side of a tree, flying headfirst over the handlebars, landing on the hard part of the dirt.

Banged up.

Bruised up.

And jacked up. I thought I was entitled to some short-term sympathy from the Mama Bear, but when she finally caught up to me the last thing on the menu was sympathy.

She looked mad. Stark raving mad with her hair swarming all around her head, hands on her hips, face twisted, lips curled upward holding firm to a pouting stance.

"What happened?" she screamed. "I told you to pedal! Not crash! Pedal goddamnit! Pedal!" she shouted in slow, grinding, overexaggerated motion.

I was mortified, standing in the back draft of her anger, which was tainted with coffee breath and the not-so-subtle whiffs of Aqua Net hair spray. And for the first time I was actually frightened of her, my mother.

Mama Bear.

Mommy dearest.

The exorcist.

Carrie.

Call her what you want, the chick was nuts!

"What happened?" she shouted so loudly that her eye sockets began to shake and roll back into her head. "What do you call that!? That was a *long* way from perfect!" she snarled. "A long, long way from perfect!"

"But I'm not perfect, Mama Bear," I said in defense of my entire six years on earth.

"Bite your tongue!" she gasped. "Let's go!" she snapped as she snatched my broken bike from the ground and with what seemed like superhuman strength or superhuman anger, she stomped all the way home with me on her heels like Lassie or Old Yeller.

How could she scream at me like this? Why hadn't she bothered to check me for cuts and contusions? *Hello. Didn't she just see me do the tango with a tree?* Instead she chose to wail, howl, and make a grand production out of an itsy-bitsy event. I wasn't trying to learn to fly the space shuttle, I was just trying to ride a bike for crying out loud. But that was no small feat to Mama Bear, it was everything. Come to think of it, *everything* was everything to Mama Bear.

There was no decent barometer for measuring stuff. Simple things became complex and everyday occurrences became chaotic. An uncomplicated show became a full-scale production and a glitch became a full-blown state of emergency. So me learning how to ride a bike at the age of six was as critical to my mother as an airline pilot learning how to land a 747 without taking out all of the passengers who had actually paid to have a seat on the plane.

Damn.

Stressful.

It was times like these that I ran to my Papa Bear. He always found a way to make me feel less like a child of my mother and more like a *normal* kid, whatever normal was.

I would sit on his lap and he would read to me from my favorite book, *Goldilocks and the Three Bears.* I had a special fondness for this particular story because Goldilocks was adventurous and bold. She seemed so free and had she not been a fictional character, I would have summoned her as my friend. I, too, wished to be bold and free like Goldilocks, but Mama Bear had her big foot on the nape of my neck and this snapped the freedom train in half at the neckline. There was also something special in the way that Papa read the Goldilocks story to me—it was the only calm part of my day and reasonable pause from my mother's mania. By the time Papa finished the story, I had begun to cry real tears while he supplied TLC to the tender spots.

"I crashed my bike today," I confessed.

"And so I heard," he said gently with one brow raised.

"Mother's really mad," I said, "isn't she."

Papa always looked around to make sure Mama was out of earshot and then he'd whisper, "Not mad. Just a little cuckoo." And then we both would laugh though we knew there was nothing funny about Mother being cuckoo all. We tried so many times to disguise my mother's obvious "imbalance" by swirling our fingers around our ears and labeling it "koo-koo."

Mama Bear made weekly visits to her therapist and frequent trips to the pharmacy to fill a bottle "to the brim" of whatever the hell it was that she needed to be kind of "normal" like the rest of us. But normal rarely lasted for long. My first day of school was a perfect example of just how abnormal she could be when unsupervised. As usual, she was jittery and impatient while driving me to school, cursing under her breath as though I were deaf.

"Get out of the way you motherfuckers!" she would yell to nonattentive pedestrians, then turn to me and smile as if she had just wished them good morning.

She'd smile and wink. I'd wink back, but when she turned

around I would roll my eyes and think, *koo-koo*. And I'd also think, *God I wish Papa were here*. I felt like I spent my whole life wishing my Papa were here. And he was here, just not *here*.

I remember the smell of Mama Bear's crisp white linen pantsuit as she escorted me across the street. I also remember her toting a white leather bag with matching white shoes. She wore a face full of makeup, which soon turned soggy when she took it upon herself to give way to the drama that she was so famous for.

"Oh God!" she suddenly began to wail at the gate as I struggled to pry my hand loose from hers. She had me in what felt like a death grip as she continued to dig deeper into her emotional outburst. That's when I began to feel marred for life— humiliated in front of people who did not know me well enough to judge me independent of the koo-koo woman who had given birth to me.

"Oh God, I just can't bear it," she mumbled and stumbled about. This elegant woman with such a pristine look was making a bumbling fool of herself in front of all my potential playmates. The boys snickered as they walked past my mother, whose dripping mascara made her eyes look like those of a raccoon. The girls looked on in awe that someone her age could act up so.

"Mama Bear," I whispered almost in a panic. "It's okay," I said. "I'll be home before dinner." *Now that wasn't funny*. Or should I say it wasn't funny enough for my mother to start laughing, cackling, and howling so inappropriately that I knew she had gone well beyond the limit of my living down her behavior.

"You are my perfect angel, aren't you? My perfect little angel and I love you so," she declared, kissing me on the forehead, smearing red lipstick across my forehead like a faded tattoo. By now I had come to despise the word *perfect* and knew that if there was such a thing as perfection, I wanted no part of it.

"I'll be here when the last bell rings!" she yelled. "I'll be standing right here!"

I smiled, then turned away and rolled my eyes, almost sprinting toward my classroom, hoping to seek refuge from the emotionally unstable woman otherwise known as my mother.

"I love you!" she yelled at the top of her lungs. "I love you so much!"

"Love you too," I replied under great obligation. It wasn't that I didn't love her or accept her love, it was just that her love came with so much drama it felt more like a burden than a joy.

By the time I entered the third grade, life had gotten complicated—really, really complicated. I was maturing rapidly, though I was still a long way from a driver's license and a legal sip of alcohol.

I no longer saw my parents as the Mama Bear and Papa Bear, but finally came to see them as people.

Flawed people.

One night while Papa was reading my favorite bedtime story, I saw sadness hovering around him. It had been there for some time now, but in recent days, weeks, or months, it had really began to manifest.

"Papa?" I questioned.

"Yes," he replied.

"Are you sad?"

"No," said his lips, but his eyes said *yes*.

"You look sad," I said challenging him.

"Not sad," he said. "Just tired." And with that Papa closed *Goldilocks* midstory and sat the book down on the floor. He mechanically kissed me on the cheek, turned out the lights, and slammed my bedroom door.

Papa?

What the hell?

Nothing had happened, but something *had* happened, because Papa was changing. Or maybe Papa had already changed. But there was no justifiable cause for change because nothing had happened. But maybe at the end of the day that in and of itself was the problem. As the weeks progressed, Papa Bear seemed to take up residency inside a well of sadness that he never ventured far from.

He stopped reading me bedtime stories.

He stopped being in touch.

He stopped being a silent buffer for my mother's madness.

One day he just up and stopped.

As my father regressed, my mother decompressed, taking to her bedroom for hours upon end listening to opera and staring into space. Still frames of her staring at the walls with tears running down her cheeks are what I remember most about the days that lead up to our Armageddon.

Mother was constantly exasperated because Father had begun missing his curfews. And then there were nights where he almost skipped coming home altogether.

"I can't take it anymore!" I heard my mother cry out on one such occasion, waking me from sleep. "Do you know what time it is? Four A.M.!!! Where have you been, Sergio? Where have you been?" she demanded.

"Taking a holiday from you," slurred Papa, cutting Mother's heart to shreds.

"What's happening to you, Sergio? Don't you love me still?"

Don't you miss me?

Don't you care?

Don't I matter?

Silence.

Silence.

And more silence. Papa had stopped answering those questions a long time ago. I do believe my mother had finally worn him down and out. She had successfully managed to push him out of love with her.

Papa turned dark overnight. I don't know, maybe it was a long time coming and neither one of us saw it. He didn't need us anymore because he had a new friend. His first name was Jack and his last name was Daniel's. And whatever the situation was with him and Jack, this would be the last night Papa would come home late. Matter of fact, this would be the last time Papa would ever come home again. And I would go from a child to an adult in less than one night and then I'd go from crazy to sane in even less than that.

"I want you out of my house!" screamed my mother to my father. "Get out of my house!"

"I paid for every damn thing in this house!" Papa yelled back, slurring his words. "Everything!"

Oh Papa, I thought. He sounded so unlike himself. His manhood had peeled away with time.

"I don't know who you are anymore, Sergio! But I want you out of this house! Out! Out! Out!" she insisted, pulling his clothing from the drawers, throwing it onto the floor. She raced madly into the kitchen to collect several large trash bags and began transferring the clothes from the floor to a bag.

"I want you out of here before sunrise! I want you out of here before my child wakes up and realizes her father is useless!"

Too late, Mother.

I had already realized too much. And as I stood at the entryway of their bedroom *and* their demise, I was reduced to tears as I watched my father stand against a wall while my mother continued to pummel him with insults.

"You ain't shit, Sergio!"

"Ain't never been shit!"

"Ain't never gonna be shit!" she said with words that leaped from her lips with a fiery edge.

Pow!

And just like that he socked her. Laid one good punch across her face and shut her down for good. I was horrified, evidenced by my eyes growing wider. Mother grabbed her face and began to scream. I held onto my own face as I also began to scream.

I will never forget the look on my father's face that night. He looked truly horrified by what he had become. He retained just enough sanity to know he had succumbed to being crazy. He looked at my mother and then at me, and back to my mother. He quickly gathered his car keys and fled the scene. He started his automobile with great urgency and backed wildly out of the driveway, burning rubber as he took off.

My mother went into the bathroom, closed the door, and began running water, probably to pour all over her face, or perhaps to drown herself in. I wasn't sure which.

I stood outside the door for six, seven minutes, almost hypnotized by the sound of running water before coming back to myself and retreating to my bedroom. I pulled out *Goldilocks and the Three Bears* and began to read it aloud, but it just didn't sound right anymore, so I threw it in the trash. Perhaps this foreshadowed how drastically my own life was about to change. I had a feeling that part of my life was done. It was the part where I had the extraordinary privilege of having a father once upon a time.

At 7:42 A.M. that same morning someone knocked on our front door. My mother and I were simultaneously shaken from our sleep only to find ourselves meeting in the hallway. She looked at me, tired and worn, with a fresh black eye, courtesy of my "gentle-natured" papa.

We did not speak.

She led.

I followed.

Two policemen stood at the door.

Waiting.

I could almost smell the blood on their shoes as they lay in wait to ruin the rest of our lives.

I was instructed to wait in my bedroom, but of course I disobeyed and hid around the corner so I could listen. But sometimes we do not like the things we are privy to hear when we do. Things like a police officer announcing to my mother that Papa had been killed in a collision this morning shortly after 4:30 A.M.

My mother collapsed, and I do believe that at that precise moment, she lost what was left of her mind. One of the policeman caught her, but he wasn't close enough to catch me. I had collapsed, too, but no one knew it because I collapsed while standing up and quite still. Amazingly, I didn't even cry, at least not right away. I shed a few tears, but not many. I couldn't fall apart because my mother was hanging off the deep end of ocean and needed constant emotional support.

Damn.

I opted to shut down my heart and go dormant instead.

Oh, Papa, how could you leave me to deal with the koo-koo woman alone? In an instant, he withdrew his bid from my world and my mother would have to replace him.

Oh God.

And this, dear reader, was my genesis.

2

BYE-BYE, VIRGIN GIRL

My mother sat me down at the kitchen table.

"Your father rode off into the sunset," she said with one sad eye and one black-and-blue one. "Just like the old movie stars." And that's how she broke the news of my father's death.

What the hell?

"So he's dead," I said bluntly, trying to shock her into reality. I didn't do it to be cruel. I was just trying to push her in the direction of being normal. I was tired of old movie stars and sunsets. I was sick to death of opera and drama. But it was bad timing because I had waited too long. I had waited till she was officially mental before insisting that she be sane. So, after my insensitive "he's dead" declaration, she burst into tears at the table where we sat.

I tried to comfort her, and she tried to comfort me.

Let's back that up . . .

She didn't try to comfort me at all because she couldn't. My mother became a walking Froot Loop in white leather heels.

Sergio! She cried out night after night from her bedroom.

Oh, Sergio!

I loved you so!

I loved you so!

She would wail and moan from her bedroom, pacing the floor in a white, transparent nightgown. Her grief encapsulated her existence, and she began to look as crazy as she sounded.

Sergio!

I loved you so!

Why did you ride off into the sunset without me?

Wasn't this the same woman who put all of his earthly belongings into a trash bag and kicked him out of the house not so long ago?

Come back to me, Sergio!

Come back.

She would fall apart in grocery stores and shopping malls. She would hang off my shoulders and throw all of her weight onto me because she "just couldn't bear it anymore!"

And I did what every good child does—sucked it up and held it in.

Compassion toward my mother wasn't my strong suit, because everything she did was an irritation. Deep down inside I probably blamed her for my father's passing. Had she not thrown him out that morning, maybe he'd still be here, what little of him there was left to be. But I couldn't attack her because she was already so frail and pitiful. If I told her that I thought she was the reason Papa was dead, she would probably spontaneously combust and ash would spew all over the Rocky Mountains. So I let her be. And I held her hand when she was scared.

And I rubbed her back when she was restless. I made her coffee in the morning and hot tea at night. And when she finally drifted off to sleep, I would retreat to my room so I could glance out of the window and count stars. I was looking for one that I could actually recognize as my Papa.

Surprisingly, I adjusted to my father's departure quickly. I never said I *liked* it, just said I adjusted. Eased into it and somehow came to make peace with his death, unlike my mother, who fought it tooth and nail. She battled my father's demise to the point where it had begun to make her old and gray before her time.

I missed Papa but I did not grieve him. Frankly, I didn't have time to grieve, because my mother was so goddamned needy. And the truth be told, our eighteen-hundred-square-foot home was just too small to accommodate her pain *and* my pain. So I let her have free reign as the "grieving widow" and I adopted the recurring role as the "resilient child." When people would ask my mother how I was taking my father's death, she always told them, "She bounced back quick."

Whatever, Mother.

Whatever.

As cruel and unfair as life seemed, there was a bright spot at the end of the muddy journey. And that would be *time*. And it was time that granted me the greatest gift of all, an emotional pardon to move on with my life. And eventually my combustible mother moved on as well.

She transferred her guilt and grief into America's two favorite pastimes: God and religion. And somewhere around my eleventh birthday, she got "saved" in the House of the Lord, transforming into a completely different person the moment the greasy preacher pushed on her forehead and knocked her backward. She accepted a part-time position in the House of the Lord as the new church secretary.

She stopped cursing.

She stopped "pining" for my father.

She stopped falling apart in public.

She stopped crying every night.

She stopped drinking coffee. Not sure why.

She stopped stopping midsentence and staring into space.

Her Christianity was a welcome change, and it would have been all good and fine if "I" weren't expected to participate in her salvation, but you just *know* that I was.

I, however, chose to maintain my stance as a religious rebel. I wasn't Rosemary's baby or anything, just felt like I was a long, long way from heaven and God. I was a fleshly girl who for whatever reason began to feel a little more worldly with the passing of each day. And it was during this critical point in my life that I was introduced to my sexuality, which emerged almost entirely by accident.

One night my mother left me under the supervision of a sixteen-year-old girl from our church because she had an overnight retreat with the old broads from her women's group. Once the adults left, this "good little Christian" babysitter put in a 911 call to her boyfriend. No sooner had the church van pool turned the corner, then the boyfriend spun onto our street from the opposite direction.

Granted, I was supposed to be sleeping, but ever since Papa died, I had learned to sleep with one eye open so as to keep a vigil over my mother to make sure she didn't do something off-beat, like accidentally stab herself to death in her sleep. Or worse, accidentally stab me to death. Therefore, I was wide awake when the babysitter's boyfriend arrived, and I'll swear before God that the babysitter doubled as a porn star. She put on the show of a lifetime right in the middle of my mother's living room on the good couch (which, by the way, I never sat on again after their little production). And of course I felt compelled to watch the event from the hallway, paying close attention to the technique and exchange.

Hips swaying.

Breasts bouncing.

Ass spanking.

Oral gratification.

What was really going on here?

"I love you!" the girl gasped. "Tell me you love me back," she demanded. "Tell me!"

There was moaning.

Groaning.

And grinding.

"Tell me you love me, baby!" she said to him.

He still didn't say anything. Then the "church girl" dropped down on two knees and put his "you-know-what" into her mouth. She started sucking and he started moaning and twisting.

"I love you!" he yelled.

I love you.

23

Love you.

Love you.

"Oh," I whispered under my breath as the picture became clearer. If this was love, then I was destined to make its acquaintance. I learned that night that I could give sex to get love and that every breathing thing with a dick would be willing to give love to get sex. Gosh, I hadn't felt love in so long I was willing to make the trade. I will give you my sex if you will give me your love. I was glad to know that love was still on the market. And I came to realize that night that if I could work it like the church ho, then maybe, just maybe, one day I would feel love again. Love that I felt when Papa was alive. Love that once upon a time I had taken for granted. I always assumed there would be at least one person who would be persuaded to love me by default or genetics, but when Papa expired, it seemed as though the universe sucked up all the love in my life, right alongside my papa's last breath.

Good Nelly, what an uneven trade. I was delivered to my birth mother, who never seemed to move beyond her own reflection in the mirror to love someone outside of herself. After Papa died, Mother became the center of the solar system and no one faulted her for it. After all, she was the grieving widow, right? In the interim, I never knew I could be so hungry for love. I would have never imagined how starved for it I would become.

The next several months bound me in a precarious position. Mother Nature grabbed me by the back of the neck and snapped me to attention, making me painfully aware of my changing body. I was banging down the doors of adolescence, egged on by raging hormones; trying to pay attention to Mother's rules and restrictions and give just due to the Lord's Holy Bible, all in the same breath. Now that sounds crazy, even to a sane person, doesn't it? Kindly insert the word *conflict* here, because there was no way I belonged in all of those places at once.

I had kick.

Gusto.

Fever.

Attitude.

Flavor.

And now, at the age of thirteen, I even had sex appeal. But of course this was grossly misinterpreted by my pathetically overzealous mother.

Ugh.

Sundays belonged to the Lord.

Jesus had become my mother's best friend. Unfortunately, I wasn't that deep. At this point, my best friends were the stash of nudie magazines I hid under my mattress sporting naked black men with six-packs. I would lay on my back and hallucinate about them. The fantasies were always the same, sexual in nature. The key players were always consistent: *me* and a beautiful, obscenely bulging, ripped, sculpted, slightly unobtainable male unlike any you have ever seen and never seen.

And of course, by the end of each delusion he would pledge undying love to me, rip himself from heaven and earth, and flee to an undiscovered world where the two of us would be joined at the hip and granted immortality to feast on fleshly desires. These beautiful men became a necessity in my life, not because I knew them but because I *needed* them.

I hit puberty so hard it hit me back.

From that moment on I had two obsessions: men and masturbation.

Masturbation. The naughty little *M*-word no one wanted to talk about. I discovered the big "*M*" at the age of thirteen. One night tension and friction met, created an explosion known as orgasm, and I was hooked.

The church said *no no* to masturbation. Shame on those sinners who sought to disrupt their erotic zones. The church told me to let those zones lay dormant.

"Sorry, Jesus, I'm afraid of decay," I confessed in my daily prayers.

The days of Goldilocks and her silly bears were gone forever. I was stone-cold addicted to *men*.

I dreamt about them.

Lusted for them.

Ached for them.

I could smell them a mile away and taste them in my sleep. But I wasn't crazy with my obsession. I *said* I was addicted, I didn't say I was an addict.

Once my mother became devoted to the Holy Roller lifestyle, I practically lived in church for the remainder of my childhood and spent most of my evenings juggling Bible studies, potlucks, and revival meetings. Religion was difficult for me because my spiritual hunger never quite developed to the magnitude of my desire for tight butts and big, soft lips.

I didn't date because courtship was not an acceptable form of recreation to my mother, especially at my age. I couldn't receive phone calls from the opposite sex because my mother viewed it as "unnecessary exchange." I didn't mingle or linger in the company of men or boys because "young women didn't carry on like that."

The best I could do was bring flash cards of naked men with me to church, strategically place them in my Bible, and when the congregation shouted for Jesus, I shouted for Mr. January, May, and December.

Amen.

Amen.

Amen.

I lost my virginity to a choirboy at the age of fourteen.

It wasn't a deep exchange.

He was cute.

Male.

And owned a penis.

My first experience was awkward.

Awkward meaning: not cozy.

It wasn't cozy because we did it in the church's bathroom stall—two feet by two feet.

I put my two feet here.

And he put his two feet there.

And this translated into just enough room for him to put his "you-know-what" where. I didn't love him, but I had sex with him because I wanted him to love *me*.

And because I was curious.

And because I wanted to connect to something more than myself.

And because I couldn't find one good reason not to anymore.

"Tell me you love me!" I demanded as his hand slid beneath my Sunday school best. "Tell me!" I insisted.

"I like you," he said without grand emotion.

Well, damn, maybe he didn't hear me.

"Tell me you *love* me," I repeated, agitated.

"I like you, Michael . . . damn," he snapped.

Like and love were two different things, so I pushed him off me and sliced the vibe in half.

"What's up, Michael?" he asked with a sigh.

"I can't believe you don't love me," I had the nerve to say.

"I don't even know you," he said throwing up his hands. In retrospect, what could I expect from a fourteen-year-old virgin choirboy?

"But I could," he said with a shy grin.

"Could what?" I asked like a wide-eyed child. "Love me?"

"Get to know you," he said sincerely.

And that was good enough for me. I felt like it had been a lifetime since anyone really wanted to know *me*. Mother never wanted to know me because she had spent a lifetime trying to know herself, and Papa fell out of love with me when he hooked up with Jack Daniel's.

Enough said.

And with that I put his hand back to where it was before and at that moment I transcended naïveté, never to own it again.

The choirboy covered my mouth with his hand because penetration hurt. But it only hurt till it began to feel *good*, which didn't take long at all.

He encouraged me to rock my hips.

He showed me how.

And I rocked and rocked, so much so that I in turn had to cover *his* mouth because he was beginning to moan and breathe too heavy. He started moving with me and we had to take turns covering each other's mouths lest we disturb the *good Christians* next door.

As the choirboy opened my hole on the bottom, he closed the hole on top, primarily the one in my heart. And for the first time in a long time I felt human *and* whole.

No longer in the company of the Virgin Mary, I arched my back and just let go. I exploded on top of the choirboy that Sunday morning. He exploded, too, but inside of me, and of course I freaked "after the fact" because we didn't use a condom.

I waited on pins and needles that month for a period.

It was the longest month of my life, but when I finally saw that dark splotch of brown smeared on the crotch of my white underwear, that was the closest thing to salvation I had ever witnessed.

Let the church say amen to that.

Amen.

Amen.

On the flip side there was guilt, not much, but some. I knew that Jesus and my mother wanted me to save myself for marriage, but it just didn't work out like that. From that moment on sexuality became my choice of expression, though I had to disguise it in Sunday suits, leotards, and hard black shoes.

Bye-bye, virgin girl.

Bye-bye.

The choirboy and I did it many more times over the course of the next year and a half, somewhere between the shuffle from church to Sunday school. He never really got to know me and I never fell in love, but that wasn't enough to keep us out of the bathroom stall every Sunday.

This was the beginning of my sexuality and the introduction of womanhood. But more than any of those things, this was the genesis of my crave.

3

FISH OUT OF WATER

I was a fish out of water, but my life was about to change. It *had* to change, because everything in the dark eventually does a slow crawl to the light. Every symphony must be played even if it falls upon deaf ears. Every poet must pursue his own verse, and every writer must make love to the world he has chosen to create. And with all of those truths foregoing, every fish must find its own true pond to swim in. At least that's what my best friend, Molly, always said.

Completely opposite in every fathomable way, Molly and I met after Papa died. We were both about ten years old. I first laid eyes on her on the school playground. She was a standout: leggy, blonde, and pretty. The new kid on the block, she was a wild child, too cool to associate with the rest of the girls, calling them "little bitches" at random.

"What's your name?" I remembered asking her.

"Molly Wood," she spat without enthusiasm, arms crossed and a bad attitude.

"So you're the new girl?" I asked, trying to be cool.

"Whatever," she said.

"Back at you," I retorted because I could be a "little bitch," too.

"You don't look like a Michael," she said.

"You don't look like a Molly."

"Whatever," she replied again.

"Do you know any other words besides *whatever*?" I asked sarcastically.

"Fuck off. Kiss my ass. And go to hell," she retorted, "but most people don't respond to my extended vocabulary."

My eyes doubled in size and it was at that moment that Molly Wood stole my heart forever, not because she was elegant or well versed, but because she was *real*.

We had nothing in common, but something had brought us together. Two lonely kids without a centerpiece whose internal abyss was so vast and deep that it bound us together for life.

I was always crazy about Molly, but growing up in the isolated world of my mother's house, I was told to curb my enthusiasm for the wild child my mother always referred to as "trailer park trash."

My mother disliked Molly intensely and I was unable to sugarcoat her disapproval. She couldn't hang out at my house, nor was I allowed to visit hers.

Mother said it was because she didn't love the Lord, but I always thought it was more because:

- Molly was white.
- She was an academic underachiever.

- Her breasts developed early.
- She was the by-product of a dysfunctional environment *(but weren't we all?)*.

My mother had no tolerance for such inconsistencies in one's life. "Bad associations spoil useful habits," she would say, and Molly Wood was considered the premier of bad associates. That's not to say that I didn't understand her concern. I just didn't always appreciate it. Actually, I understood better than anyone, because I was privy to the uncensored world of Molly Wood, and the girl was definitely no choirgirl.

Molly bored easily and her signature statement, "Let's blow this Popsicle stand," often defined her journey. She lived and died by one rule: "Go sideways till you run out of room. Then jump, fall, crash, or burn, but whatever you do, don't go straight, don't ever go straight, because straight will only lead you to ordinary."

Sometimes we would cut class and hide out in the girl's bathroom, sit on the floor, and philosophize.

"Michael, there's only one thing worse than being dead," Molly always said.

"What's that?"

"Being ordinary," was always her final answer. "And if you chose to be ordinary," Molly added, "have the guts to do the shit extraordinarily."

I spent most of my childhood in awe of Molly because she was vivacious, worldly, and free. She was so unlike me, ultraconservative and on lockdown in the House of the Lord. I marveled at the way she did life, and listening to her wild stories of sex and chaotic orgies made me want to lay down with every choir boy in town.

One day while in the ninth grade, we ditched school so we could spend half the day smoking weed down by the river. Notice I said *half* the day. The other half was spent airing out my skin, hair, and disposition lest Mother discover that Michael Morgan liked to get high. And it was on such a day that I came to acknowledge the brutal truth about other people's lives. Rarely do we accurately summarize other people's journey without squeezing ourselves into the full length of their journey.

It was common knowledge that Molly lived with a foster mom because her father was a deadbeat and her mother was dead. I had always wondered exactly what happened to Molly's mother, until one day I got brave enough to ask.

"What happened to your mother?"

"Gone," she said.

"Gone?" I asked naively.

"Crazy," she said flatly.

"What made her crazy?" I asked.

After a long pause she whispered, "*Me.*"

Once I saw the tears swell in her eyes and begin to fall against the backdrop of her sad expression, I no longer wanted to be Molly. *Being her just wasn't easy anymore.*

"We can get off this topic," I suggested, because I didn't want to make Molly uncomfortable in pursuit of a full-blown analysis of nutty mothers.

"Good," Molly retorted, obviously not wishing to drag up the past. But then she came right back to it and that was typical Molly. *Always* expect the unexpected.

"She borrowed a shotgun from a friend and one day while I was in English class, she blew her head clear off her body."

"Molly," I gasped reaching for her hand, but she pulled away.

"No big fucking deal," Molly said harshly. "She was a loser."

I didn't know what to say. Sometimes it was best to say nothing until something sensible came along. And perhaps this is why we both sat in silence for a long, long time.

"Tell me about your mother," Molly demanded anxiously.

I nodded, twitched, and shifted, suddenly feeling awkward myself.

"She's different," I said.

"What does different mean?" Molly asked.

"Annoying," I quickly replied. "She's a Jesus freak . . ."

"So what does that mean?" Molly asked.

"Nothing, just a lot of extra demands," I said flatly.

"So she expects a lot from you?"

"Not a lot," I said. "Just perfection."

Perfection.

Now that was something we would both have to learn along the way. That thing I coined as "perfection" that day fell somewhere between the cracks, sidewalks, reservoirs, and dams. It hid under intrinsic things like birth defects and hearts with holes. We would never know perfect, Molly and I. And our lives, our friendship, and our love would be anything but perfect, or ordinary for that matter.

Molly and I remained friends throughout high school. I even managed to schedule frequent trips between choir practice and Bible studies during our formative teenage years to hang with her down by the river.

We would sit on the edge of muddy banks and contemplate the meaning of life over a bag of Cheetos and a stash of marijuana. Our friendship wasn't the deepest in the world, but it did manage to have great meaning. It meant a lot to my sanity knowing there was at least one other person in the world who missed the mark of "perfection" as much as I did.

"What do you want to be when you grow up?" I often asked Molly when we were young. And she never had an answer, just posed the question back to me, "What do you want to be?"

"Free," I would respond. "That's what I want to be." She would always shake her head at my answer.

"What?" I would ask defensively.

"Free?" she asked sarcastically. "Why are you asking for so much?"

"What?" I asked, puzzled by her reply.

"You want to be free?" she asked, staring up at the sky. "Free is huge," she said. "You might as well ask to be God or something . . . free?" she asked again.

I started laughing because only Molly Wood would see freedom as an impossibility, and the irony of that was she was the freest person I knew. Perhaps she was free because she knew freedom was unobtainable to most mortals.

"Well at least I have some idea of what I want to be when I grow up," I said boasting on one such occasion down by the river.

"Oh," she said calmly. "I know what I want to be when I grow up."

"Well you never said . . ."

"Just because I didn't tell you doesn't mean I didn't know," I said.

"Well . . ." I said with attitude. "Spill it. What do you want to be when you grow up?"

She turned to me and looked with such seriousness that I was waiting for an earth shattering declaration of her adulthood.

"Well?" I asked on the edge. "What do you want to be?"

"Tall," she said.

And wouldn't you know it? Molly Wood grew up to be six feet one inches tall, fitted with insane curves and silicone. She took it upon herself to adopt the ways of people of color, with the only obvious glitch in her soulful demeanor: bleached blonde hair and baby-blue eyes.

She spent most of her adulthood in and out of rehab due to her love-hate relationship with cocaine. Molly Wood had taken up the oldest profession in the world, and her life was a theatrical production. There were the majors and the minors, the supporting cast and the enablers. There were the codependents and the addicts and all of the flesh-and-bone people who offered nothing more than background scenery and bad influence.

And though I continued to love her deeply, she drifted away to a different part of the sea. I never judged Molly. I just put some distance between us for comfort's sake.

I understood that cocaine was Molly's suitor and the only viable option for all that she lacked. Molly never loved anything more than her coke, and that is why she would always return to it without fail or apology. And at any given moment she could be found straddling the crack pipe and a strange man's privates, all in the name of escaping this great illusion called *life*.

I in turn grew up into my own sense of whatever the hell it was that I was supposed to be.

Twenty-nine years into this thing called life.

Single.

Progressive.

Functional.

Did I mention *single* already?

By trade I became a beautician. I beautify dead people, so I guess one could say cadavers are my livelihood. I fell in to this line of work by mistake after taking a "temporary" job as a receptionist the year I graduated from high school. I wound up staying longer than anticipated (*most of us do*), and when an advancement opportunity presented itself, I jumped at it lest I find myself at the edge of a dead-end job (no pun intended) going nowhere.

I refer to myself as a trend setter. I'm simple, but not so simple that I can't get your attention and *keep* it. I don't carry enough presence to command the statement, "I'm the girl you want to be," but I do command enough to say, "I'm the girl you want to be *like*."

I'm not drop-dead gorgeous, but if I were walking down the street, you might look twice. Twice to get a second look at my thighs, legs, and hips swaying to the beat of an invisible wind. And to dissect the motion of these disarming curves.

I wear my hair in a bob and I lighten it for affect, not effect. My skin is caramel and my eyes can't decide if they want to be gray or green. I wear tight clothing because I can get away with it. But then again, I could be nothing more than a caricature created by a horny man in a desperate hour.

At the end of the day, when it was all said and done, no matter how intense my passion for the extraordinary, I've always been a good girl, on the exterior anyway.

My mother had an obsession for perfection, and somehow I always tried to deliver on time and under budget, despite my handicap in the situation. Bubble burst for the day: *I'm not so perfect after all*, but after Papa died, I stepped up to the plate and became so in many ways. I caught my mother's dreams and kept them in my back pocket, even the ones that I knew would be impossible to fulfill.

"I want you to be a movie star," she used to say when I was young. And then after Papa died she wanted a doctor in the family because "a doctor could have saved his life." When she turned to religion for salvation, she changed her mind yet again and wanted me to be a missionary for the Lord. But by the time I turned twenty-nine and was still unwed all she really wanted me to be was married.

I didn't want to hurt or disappoint my mother, but I just I didn't have the heart to tell her that the perfect me she loved really wasn't *me* at all. In many ways, my mother never saw me because she was long gone, lost in the dream of what she hoped

I would become. But Mother never knew what I dreamt about because she dictated my dreams as an extension of herself. If she knew what I dreamt about she would have performed an exorcism on me. She would have also washed my mind out with soap.

Dirty girl.

Dirty girl.

Oh no, Mother had no idea as to the severity of my dreams. And let's face it—it was probably a lot easier for her to transfer her dreams on to me than for her to actually expend an ounce of ambition to try and obtain them herself.

Movie star.

Emergency room doctor.

Missionary.

Married.

Whatever, Mother.

In many ways, I was my mother's keeper right up until the day I moved out. I stayed home a ridiculous amount of time, almost thirty years before moving. I never intended on staying so long, but I didn't want my mother to be alone. She never dated after Papa died, and who could blame her? Where in the world could she find someone to replace him?

"Why don't you stay a little longer?" she begged while standing at the entry of my bedroom, watching me pack my last bag.

Twenty-nine years wasn't long enough? I wanted to shout, but couldn't bring myself to be that rude.

"I'm not comfortable with you living alone," she said, but that was far from the truth. She wasn't comfortable with *herself* living alone and it was just as easy to pretend that it was all about me, for a change of pace.

"I won't be far away," I reassured her. "Just a few miles up the road."

"You'll be farther than you think," she said solemnly.

Yes, I know, I wanted to cry out with jubilation. The farther the better. There would be no more sneaking to meet men to satisfy my cravings. No more heavy plotting to find a place to do some heavy petting. No more getting busy in the backseat because *everybody* was living at home.

"Mother, please don't guilt-trip me," I begged. "For once, just be happy for me," I pleaded.

Mother smiled and for a moment I thought she was going to break with kindness and wish me well, but before I could catch a kind word her mouth curled upward giving way to a frown. It was a frown so bitter that it frightened me.

My heart dropped.

"Don't forget to lock up on your way out!" she snapped, exiting to her bedroom where she slammed the door hard. And my heart dropped again upon its closure. And that was my mother, ladies and gentlemen. She would always have a flair for theatrics.

Like I said at the onset, there are countless numbers of people who walk around each day with a gaping hole in the middle of their heart, and as a result they leak.

And long.

Need.

Ache.

And crave.

Desperately struggling to cover.

Shade.

And conceal the monster that drives their every impulse toward "the one" who will deliver them from evil. And this is where the real story begins with Molly Wood on hiatus (read between the lines: in rehab again) and me after the discovery of my first gray hair.

4

A DEAR JESUS LETTER

I'm aging by the minute.

I recently found my first gray pubic hair and freaked completely out. I am confident that I had certifiable reason to freak because gray vaginal hair is definitely in the "freak zone."

Pardon my hysteria, but I have no one to commiserate with on my miseries. My best friend is in detox, and I am ill at ease to discuss anything below the waist with my mother.

But I am scared.

Really scared.

It's one gray pube today, an entire gray snatch tomorrow.

Upon radar detecting my first gray pube, the center of gravity shifted, settling somewhere within the confines of my female genitalia.

Michael Morgan is aging.

And melting.

Michael Morgan is human.

And mortal.

Don't you get it? I am running out of time to find love. With the subtle transformation of each black hair to gray, how much longer can I stay in the race? It was this discovery that sent me ahead of myself and propelled me full throttle into a series of one-night stands, or marathon dating as I liked to call it.

I didn't set out to have so many transfers and exchanges. I wasn't on a mission to have the highest number of returns. I never intended to be a sperm receptacle, it just sort of happened that way. When I moved out of my mother's house my life began to feel like a free-for-all-fuck-fest reunion. But not because I was a slut or fast, it was more along the lines of emergency and panic.

Red alert!

Red alert!

Gray pubic hair in the house!

My situation frightened me to the point where I felt the need to sit down and write Jesus a letter and bring him current on the state of my pathetic affairs.

Dear Jesus,

Gerry didn't work out because Gerry didn't work. And after spending one night in complete darkness because "pretty didn't pay the light bill," Gerry and I broke up and are no longer speaking.

Marshall wasn't a viable suitor because when he finally revealed himself to me, I found that his breasts were larger than mine because he used to be a she. Once I regained consciousness, Marshall informed me that his real name was Michelle and he/she was in the midst of surgically altering his/her gender. Marshall and I are no longer speaking.

Quintone was my black knight in the third grade. He promised one day to ride up to my bedroom window bareback on a beautiful white horse. Quintone was a man of his word, and twenty years later we re-united when he rode up to my window on the back of a mule. Jesus, there was only one problem with this little scenario: I couldn't figure out which one was the mule. The very next day I moved because some things are just too scary for real life.

Rashid and I were soul mates for sure. I met him one night at a poetry reading. The moment our eyes locked I knew he was the "It Man." We were drawn to one another like fire catches to dry brush. And had he not been arrested the following week and sent back to jail for violation of parole, I would have made a lifelong commitment to him. But unfortunately given the current climate, I had to move on. Obviously, Rashid and I are no longer speaking.

William was a man after my own heart. He had all of his teeth, or so I thought. But one steamy night after a long, passionate kiss, I pulled back to take a break and his teeth came with me. I politely returned his teeth to him, mouthed the words "bye-bye," and changed my phone number the next day.

Keith could have been the one. I met him at a taco stand, and I was certain he was the "It Man." He was beautiful, articulate, and one of my favorite things on earth, employed. He was the personification of everything I wanted in a man. He owned his own mind, body, and soul. A Yale graduate, he embodied a scholarly quality that I was rather fond of. When I was in his presence he felt like the last man on earth. The first time I laid eyes on him, I fell inside his dreamy eyes like a one-dimensional character found in poorly written romance novels. But on our first date I became extremely irritated by this simple fact: his wife kept paging him during our meal.

Good night, Keith.

Jesus, those were the weirdoes, but not every man bordered on strange or the supernatural. There were plenty of well-seasoned, charming, likable gentlemen with faces that did not resemble animal parts. There were dozens who held down real jobs and lived normal lives. They drove respectable cars and engaged in stimulating conversation. They paid their rent each month because having a roof over their head gave them a "natural high."

Their walking shoes were filled with dreams, which carried them down the road less traveled. As a matter of fact, the road was so less traveled I didn't even know where the hell it was. As a result, I never found my prince. One day I awoke only to realize that the nice guys, eligible bachelors, potential mates, and possible soul mates had disappeared.

Farewell, sweet prince.

Good night.

I shall weep your departure because all that's left behind are the guys with big bellies and bad credit, character flaws and cash-flow problems. Guys that can't formulate two sentences without the phonics game. Guys who would be homeless if it weren't for that back bedroom their mothers forgot to give away to someone more deserving.

So, Jesus, in lieu of how sorry for me I know you must feel by now, I am down on my knees begging for mercy. I ask for an eligible, employed, nonviolent single man with no current wives or husbands who has more teeth than felony convictions to enter my world and escort me to the rest of my life. Amen.

I wrote Jesus that letter and mailed it to him several days ago, but I still do not believe he has received it yet.

5

THE MAGIC KINGDOM

Lorenzo.

Gorgeous.

Six-five, 257½ pounds.

I weighed him on my back, on my stomach, and on my back again. I met him at the 7-Eleven at a quarter till twelve on a lonely Saturday night.

"Do you *eat*?" I asked him.

"What?"

"Do you *eat*?" I asked again.

"Do I *eat*?"

"You look to be about 250 pounds. I would assume that you *eat*."

"Oh," he said breathing relief. "Yeah."

"*Eat* with me someday," I said handing him my card.

I walked away without waiting for a reply.

I didn't have to wait.

He'd call.

"Oh shoot," I said banging my hand against the steering wheel of my car, "I gave him the wrong card."

"Shoot," again.

The card I gave him was my business card, not my play card. My play card was neon. It read: "One Day in My World Is a Lifetime in Yours."

Bbbbrrrinnnnnggggg . . .

Before I could even get in the door from the 7-Eleven the phone was ringing.

Bbbbrrrinnnnnggggg . . .

"Hello?"

"Michael?" he asked.

"Yes," I confirmed.

Guaranteed.

"Your name is *Michael?*"

"Michael," I repeated, slightly agitated.

"This is Lorenzo. I'm the guy you met five minutes ago."

"I know who you are. But what I don't know is what took you so long to call?"

He laughed.

I didn't.

He thought I was kidding.

I wasn't.

I really was waiting for the call. I was always waiting for the call from the guy who would come into my life, alter my existence, and make it better somehow. It wasn't bad, the life I was living, but I just wanted a better one.

I wanted a life with the white picket fence. I wanted three bedrooms, two and a half baths. I wanted stairs that went up, down, and all around. I wanted thick, beige, wall-to-wall carpet that sank into my feet and contemporary furniture that sank into my butt. I wanted obscure art hanging on my walls. I wanted a garage door opener and a side-by-side refrigerator filled with food. I wanted a patio with a view. I wanted lawn chairs, a gardener, and an icemaker.

I wanted waffles in the morning, popcorn at night. I wanted a sleeper sofa for guests. I wanted 2.5 kids and a VCR that worked so I could tape *Oprah* in the afternoon. And when all was said I done, I wanted someone to begin where I ended and to end where I began.

I was sick to death of dragging myself to parties *alone*. I couldn't bear to stand in the middle of Blockbuster Video one more Saturday night and pretend that I was renting movies for me and my Invisible Man.

I could not tolerate attending one more godforsaken house party, engagement celebration, holiday dinner, or wedding *dateless*. Every time I stepped outside I swore that even the clouds were gossiping about the pathetic state of my love life as they whispered to one other.

Where is her man?

She still ain't got no man?

Oh, by herself again *this year?*

I wanted history with someone, but to get history he had to stay longer than one night. I wanted to fight and argue, make up and make love. I wanted another human to experience the human experience with.

I didn't want to do *solo* anymore.

I'd done solo all of my life.

I wanted a warm body to rock me to sleep on sleepless nights. I wanted someone on the other side of my morning jog. I wanted another pair of feet down at the bottom of my bed so I could brush against them each morning and confirm I was still alive. I wanted an ear on the end of the good news and a heart on the end of the bad. I wanted a soul mate on the other end of my soul to unravel me when I rolled into a ball and wished like hell to disappear.

I didn't want a perfect life.

I just wanted a *different* one.

So, yes, I was always waiting for the call.

"I wasn't sure I wanted to call," he said.

"Really?"

"Yeah, Tucker Funeral Services?" he questioned.

"Oh," I replied laughing. "The business card."

I never gave out my business card because it read, "Beautician, specializing in the beautification of corpses."

I am a dream-weaver.

My job objective is to make the corpses look like they did when they were living. But in reality, the only way I can I make them look like they did when they were living is to bring them back to life. But since I'm not certified in resurrections, the best I can do is help them to look less bad from being dead.

Two days later Lorenzo and I had dinner. And two days after that he was standing in the middle of my bedroom in a three-piece, teal green suit. I had given him a standing invitation to my world and he took me up on the invite one evening after work. So there he was standing in my room with an essence that was so majestic that it called me to him without saying a word. God, he knew how to work it—his pretty, rich brown eyes and curly eyelashes were blowing my mind.

"Are you the *last* man?" I asked him from a distance. A distance of about five feet, from his center to my end, as I hung from my canopy bed upside down.

"Would you like me to be?" he asked coming closer.

Oh damn.

"Would you like me to be?" he asked again. "I can be whatever you want me to be," he crooned in my ear.

And I was . . .

Absolutely . . .

Breathless.

I want you to be "The One."

The "It Man."

I want you to be for real.

I want you to say what you mean and mean what you say.

I want you to be programmed with emotional integrity and

fully equipped with all the necessary wires in place for honesty. I want you to want me without makeup and double-D breasts. I want you to be sincere, compassionate, understanding, *and* employed.

I want you to be worth waiting for.

I want you to be reality and not the hallucination I created on a lonely night. I want your heart to be as flawless as your cocoa butter skin and I want your soul to be as developed as your biceps. I want your patience to be as long as your size fourteen shoe. (*What? Size fourteen?*)

I don't want you to be perfect. I just want you to be.

Now, I didn't say all of this out loud, which is why Lorenzo asked me again, "What do you want me to be?"

Dear God.

He was truly a man whose qualifications extended beyond his perfect pecs, specializing in the articulation of seduction as sex hormones oozed from his skin and dripped all over my floor.

Stop it, I wanted to say. *Stop it pleeeaaasseeee. Can't you see how weak I am? Can't you tell I'm starting to swell in places I can't mention out loud? Stop it, pleeeeaaassse.*

I was not about to let this man, this beautiful black man with an angular jaw, sculpted body, seductive eyes, bald head, toffee-colored skin, and full lips enter into my world. I was not about to let eloquent words and flawless presentation talk me out of my good sense.

"What do you need me to be?" he asked again as the brother got down on his knees and unzipped his pants.

I was holding on for dear life.

Upside down . . .

On the edge of my bed . . .

At the end of my world and grip.

Michael don't be easy, I thought to myself. *Don't fall like this again*. One beautifully sculpted naked leg kneeled beside my bed while the other was still in his pants.

"If you want more you'll have to do it yourself," he said softly.

Perspiration was forming on the base of my temples, sweating my press and curl straight out. I didn't want to hyperventilate, but I felt an uncertain need to pant.

One eye dropped toward the floor.

Okay.

Let's regroup. I could see who he was and what he represented. I could also feel what he thought and taste what he wanted, but I just couldn't go there with him. Or could I?

He unbuttoned his shirt, one seductive button at a time.

Top to bottom to bottom to bottom.

Michael don't be easy, I scolded myself again and tried to remember all of the reasons I should wait, all the reasons of my past. All the reasons that had blown up in my face time and time again and left me with my only lover, my last lover being the tired pillow I cried myself to sleep in night after night.

Michael don't be easy, I thought once again because his shirt was on the floor and the rest was coming down.

No shirt.

No tie.

No pants.

No shoes.

Just a pair of briefs stood between him and his nakedness.

I honed in on the bulge inside his briefs and tried to look away.

Michael don't be easy, I shrieked inside my skin. Don't you remember the last time, spending your last dime searching for the wreckage of your heart after what's-his-name? What's-his-name? Remember what's-his-name who left you neck-high in dusty, hot tears? Remember him? He scorched you so bad there are still blisters from what time just cannot heal. Remember the glue you couldn't find to piece together what was left of your heart after the last one and the one after that *and* the one after that? *Don't be easy, Michael.* You can't live through *that* again.

"Now, if you want more you'll have to do it yourself," he said with finality.

Kneeling he looked so submissive.

Passive.

Vulnerable.

Fragile.

Jesus, he wasn't a man. He was a God transcended into the body of a human and he was waiting to be held and rocked to sleep.

I can rock you, I thought. *Honey, I can rock you.*

"Baby," he whispered.

I don't remember if he said, "Come here," or if I said, "Here I come," but next thing I knew I was kneeling directly in front of him, more vulnerable than he *ever* could be. My hands traveled the course of his body, following his veins like a road map.

Up, down, sideways, and back around did I go, gathering his skin beneath my fingers.

Dear God, I panted. Don't let this be another dead end and something *else* I'll have to survive.

Good Nelly.

"What do you want?" he pleaded into my eyes, bled into my soul.

He kissed me softly across my breast, intercepting my zone at the nipple where he paused to suckle a moment.

My knees bent in two and down I went.

Physically.

Emotionally.

Spiritually.

Circumstantially.

And geographically.

I was down giving too much from what I had left to give. "Please," I said, asked, or begged—I don't know which it was. And before I could think about what was happening brilliantly enough to stop it, he had positioned himself on top of me; 257½ pounds of man, machine, or steel, and again I'm not sure which it was.

My legs opened automatically without hesitation, reservation, litigation, or concentration. They just did, parted like the Red Sea, and that night *all* the Israelites were set free.

Morning.

He was still there, a good sign.

I woke up first because I didn't want him to see me without preparation.

While he slept I stepped into the shower to freshen up.

I almost started singing. As a matter of fact I did start singing: "You make me feel. You make me feel. You make me feel like a natural woman." I hit the high notes and then I took the low ones.

I wanted to experience Lorenzo again.

Naked, I emerged from the bathroom, only to find him fully clothed, sitting on the edge of the bed sliding into his shoes.

My heart sank. *What's his hurry?*

"Good morning," I said trying to disguise my disappointment.

"Hey, baby," he said without looking up. "I gotta jet. I'm late for an appointment."

I stood there naked, nodding and pretending to be okay.

"Do you want coffee?" I asked trying not to sound as desperate as I was.

"No, babe, don't have time," he said.

"Oh," I mumbled, trying to beat down The Great Depression. I propped myself against a light, airy mood instead. He towered over me, offering a bland kiss on the cheek. There was no spice, nothing nice. It was the kind of kiss one would offer his mother or his priest. This was a definite departure from last night's tongue-down-the-back-of-your-throat kiss.

"I like your outfit," he said referring to my birthday suit. "Sweet."

"Thanks," I half smiled.

"I'll call you later," he said as he fled the scene like a grave robber.

But later never comes.

Later never does.

After Lorenzo left, the sound of emptiness vibrated through my house and *through* my house. I felt like an orange peel that had just been detached from its natural surface, thrown to the ground, and forgotten about. There was only one difference: I didn't have the luxury of being biodegradable.

"Again, Maxwell," I said, turning up the volume so loud the soft spots in my ears turned hard. "Whenever, wherever, whatever" sang the sexy neo-soul balladeer.

I made Maxwell sing it again and again. And although he had recorded the song years earlier in a dense studio, I was convinced that it was *my* song. That it had been composed and created especially for me. Had he been spying on me through my curtains and seen my lonely heart by mistake?

"Please, Maxwell, please," I begged him while stationing my finger on the rewind button like an addict desperate for healing. I breathed every note of "Whenever, Wherever, Whatever," inhaling every chord, swallowing it whole, holding it down deep till it escaped through the openings in the pores of my skin.

Could I breathe this lonely away? Could I breathe this lonely away, Maxwell? If I couldn't breathe it away, could I sneak up on it and suffocate it when wasn't staring at me?

L-O-N-E-L-Y visited me every now and again and sometimes it came with a duffel bag and stayed for days.

I saw L-O-N-E-L-Y against my shadow as I walked down the street, lingering on the heels of my last step, cementing in stone steps I had not yet taken. L-O-N-E-L-Y drove home with me last night and sat in the passenger's side taking in the rush-hour scene.

L-O-N-E-L-Y sat on my chest as I tried to eat my dinner and when I slipped into my bath, it beat me to the water. It was waiting on me when I crawled into the bed where it took pot-shots and ministabs at my heart, tearing into it for pleasure and selfish gain.

I watched L-O-N-E-L-Y dance in the street. It kicked dirty water between my eyes and meticulously delivered my attention to lovers holding hands in the park.

"See," lonely taunted.

"See what you're missing . . ."

"See what you can't find."

"See what you can't hold? Lorenzo's gone, too, right? Just like the others."

Years ago, I grew tired of lonely and his lament, so I chained him in a box and threw him into the bottom of the ocean. For the most part, lonely has remained chained, but sometimes he escapes, especially on holidays, when he is unsupervised. And upon his release, he *always* comes back to me.

Most people couldn't see lonely because I disguised him against pretend smiles and make-believe joviality. I shrink-wrapped him in plastic and buried him under hearty laughs and quirky jokes, but lonely was always there.

"I know you understand, Maxwell," I said turning down the volume.

I am intimate with the painful distance between the last good-bye and the next hello. I know the terms of the trade and accept it as such, one beautiful brown body in exchange for one ounce of unconditional love. I have acknowledged that forever is just a seven-letter word and all it really means is the length of time between the guy I *just* slept with and next guy, should he *ever* come along.

I was horny.

Lorenzo was there.

And L-O-N-E-L-Y.

Lorenzo was there.

I was tired of waiting for the right situation to "give it up." Honestly, deep down inside I feared the right situation would never find my address. I was sure Lorenzo was "on the level." And why wouldn't he be? He was *there*.

I needed to be held, rocked, stroked, because it had been so long since I felt that kind of closeness with another human being. And he was there, just long enough to deliver and to take away.

Now all I needed was someone to reassure me that I hadn't made a bad decision. I needed the security of knowing that I hadn't slept with him prematurely or used poor judgment *again*. I needed confirmation that I had not crossed the "ho" line yet. After all, how many had it been now?

Prince Charming won't be shocked when he finds me, the world's largest sperm receptacle. The prince won't be disappointed that my legs weren't crossed awaiting his arrival. Will he? When he finally shows, I'll have to tell him about Lorenzo and Michael, Stuart, Damian, Diego, Marcus, Troy, and the other Troy. I had gone around the rotation so many times that I was running into the same names twice. I hope the prince won't be appalled that I can't even remember the names of everyone I allowed into my Magic Kingdom. I needed my own personal dream weaver to come in, wave a wand, and put my mind at ease.

I'm still lovable, worthy, right?

I'm not cheap, not easy, right?

I gave my body, not my soul, right?

Wrong.

I had to let it go because I couldn't hold it anymore.

Tears and more tears.

And with that I summed up my momentary existence by scribbling into my diary the only two words I still had the strength to write: *I crave.*

6

LONDON BRIDGE CAME FALLING DOWN

My phone rang at 6 A.M.

I already knew who it was, and even though I was sound asleep, I answered as though I had been up all night waiting for the call. And in some ways, I was expecting the early morning disturbance, because Molly Wood rang every Monday at 6 A.M., even though the past five years I had been telling her to make it a little closer to seven.

"Hi baby," I said, trying not to sound as flatlined as I felt.

"Uh-oh," she said. "Sounds like somebody's got an ouchie. . . ." Of course, leave it to Molly to call me out, exposing the emotional lies I tried to tell. Molly was good at it—seeing stuff I never showed and hearing the things I never said.

Once upon a time, I thought she was deeply insightful; now I realized it wasn't that deep. And the only reason she was in tune with the pain that others have tried to hide is because she has been in so much of it during her lifetime. And I did not want to burden her with the weight of my dysfunction and loneliness. She had enough on her shoulders trying to stay sober, and tiny matters of the heart could drive her back to drinking. Hell, *breathing* could drive Molly back to drinking, and that's why I kept my mouth shut.

"I'm fine," I said, trying to convince myself enough to convince her. "The question is, how are you?"

"Not high enough to fly yet," she said in jest.

"Where are you?"

"Halfway house."

"How was rehab?"

"Sobering."

"So what's next, Molly Wood?"

"Broadway."

I laughed.

"Or Disneyland," she said, completing her trip down fantasy lane.

"You really okay?" I asked.

"Fucking A," she said.

"Okay," I said, not believing her any more than she believed me. "I'll see you soon, right?"

"Sooner than it takes me to fall off the wagon and end up in another detox program."

Molly laughed, but I didn't. She thought it was funny, or maybe she didn't. I didn't find any humor in Molly's addiction, only fear. As light as she always managed to make it, I knew that if she didn't get it right she would die one day. We were all going to die someday anyway, but Molly would die sooner than the rest of us if she didn't incorporate *sober* into her daily routine.

"Love you, Molly Wood," I said before signing off and hearing the same parting words she always gave me.

"Likewise," she said.

Likewise was the only way Molly could say she loved me. She didn't do love or life very well. And with the knowledge that her mother had decapitated herself on a very bad day, I never expected Molly to be "very well" at all. She consumed the pain without skipping a beat, treading water better than most learn to do it in *two* lifetimes.

She never loved too hard or breathed too deep.

She never felt too much.

Never did life grand.

She numbed herself on white powder and straight tequila shots.

And that was the real Molly Wood, in or out of rehab. She would never get too far away from being high no matter how much detox she went through.

Take care of yourself Molly Wood.

Take care of yourself, girl.

Later that morning I smelled the celestial aroma of frying bacon wafting through my home. My neighbor Sky Dobson was cooking again, and I couldn't pass up dining on the swine or a legitimate opportunity to cry on his big, strong shoulders.

I had met Sky a few months ago when I accidentally backed over his bike with my car on the day I moved into my apartment. He watched in horror from across the street where he was conversing with neighbors.

Uh-oh.

"Why did you park your bike in the street?" I raised my voice in defense as I leapt from my car to appraise the damage. Though I was shaken by the incident, I couldn't help but notice as he sprinted toward me from across the street that he was damn fine. He was every bit of six feet and some change. Bronze skin, hard, raw muscle, carved dimples, chocolate eyes, and texturized curls. Now, maybe I should stop right *there*.

"My bike was on the sidewalk and so was your car!" he said retaliating, bringing me back to the situation at hand.

"My car was on the street," I insisted.

He reached down and untangled the bike from the bumper.

"Oh, damn," I said evaluating the bike's mangled handlebars.

He looked at the bike for a moment, then shrugged. I wasn't sure if he was going to flip out, so I humbled myself, especially when a second glance confirmed that my car had indeed jumped the curb and landed on the sidewalk.

"I'll pay you for the damage to the bike," I offered, sucking it up as my fault.

"Don't worry about it," he said, sizing me up. "You look like you could use a break."

"I'm not poor or anything," I said defensively. "I can pay you for the bike."

"Hey," he said reaching for my hands, "I didn't mean anything by it."

"I'm sorry," I said, embarrassed that I had overreacted. "Can

I make it up to you? How about I cook you dinner?" I asked with a smile, which softened the tension considerably.

"Under one condition," he said.

"And that would be?"

"That you cook better than you drive," he said with a big grin.

Long story short, I burned the first meal I cooked for him and to top it off, the gas stove caught fire. But nothing bonds two people faster than burned pork chops and a grease fire. After Sky and I both survived our near-death experiences (pork chops, house fire, and plowed-down bike), we became very good friends. But surprisingly, it wasn't physical between us. Still don't know how that happened, since I found him so attractive. It just seemed that his beauty and my attraction never crossed lines at the same time. Though once upon a time, I tried like hell to merge the two.

"How do you see me?" I asked him one night while we were hanging out at his place drinking, sitting on his couch, too cozy perhaps as we rested our heads against one another.

"What do you mean?" he asked cockeyed.

Duh?

"How do I look to you?" I asked again, trying to break it down in dummy terms.

"You look fine," he said flatly.

"Define fine," I commanded.

"Normal. Two eyes. Two ears. A nose," he said pinching my nose.

Well, damn, could he make this any harder?

"Fine enough to kiss?" I asked, pushing it. I looked away for a beat and the next thing I knew, homeboy was snoring. I couldn't believe it! He fell asleep right there on my shoulder.

Well, good night to you, too. Shit. We'll see if I ask your sleepy ass anything else again.

I took that as a sign from God that we should just be friends and nothing more. After all, a beautiful male friend wasn't the worst thing in the world to have—was it? Although we maintained a consistent friendship, I always viewed him as one of my potential soul mates. And not a day had gone by that I did not long to feel him on a deeper level. But I dared not bring it up, lest the sounds of heavy snoring fill the room and hurt my feelings. *Again.*

"Come and get Miss Piggy!" Sky bellowed from the other side of the window, referencing his world-class bacon. I pressed my nose against the glass and he pressed back.

"What are you doing home today?" he said, checking his watch. He knew I should be at work by now, fixing up the dead.

"Damage control," I said sheepishly.

His smile faded to a frown.

He closed the curtain and opened the side door.

I walked in like a child stepping into the principal's office.

Sky had always objected to my getting "too close too soon," and could tell by the huge rejection banner hanging over my head that I hadn't listened.

"I really liked him . . ." I blurted, trying to stall before the "I told you so" lecture slapped me upside the head. Sky slammed the door, ignored my comment, and continued cleaning, while Dixie, his pet iguana, crawled around on the kitchen floor.

"You didn't even know him," I said, keeping one eye on the lizard's tail, making sure she kept her distance and I kept mine.

"Yeah, right," said Sky.

"I felt a connection," I said in my defense.

"You felt an erection."

"He was beautiful . . ."

"Only on the outside," he shot back while picking up Dixie and taking her into his bedroom to put her back into the cage. He reentered the kitchen, grabbed two mugs and a fresh pot of coffee, and sat them down hard on the table.

Oh, God, time for a talk.

I sat.

He stood.

I waited.

He stewed.

I tapped my fingers on the table.

He didn't say a word.

I couldn't take it anymore.

"I know what you're going to say," I blurted.

"Then tell me, because I sure as hell don't!" he snapped.

This was an uncomfortable conversation, because I was still remotely attracted to Sky as well.

I felt as though I was standing directly beneath Niagara Falls and still I couldn't get wet. The falls were raging, throbbing, and exploding around me, but not one spitting drop would have the decency to land on my torch-burned skin and put out these urgent flames.

I want you so bad, so bad Sky. And I want you even worse right now because I feel so rejected by Lorenzo. I wish you could take away this pain and wash me clean with your scent by replacing his.

We walked from the kitchen to the bedroom. Sky stretched out on the bed and turned on CNN. His hands rested on top of a naked chest dented with muscle.

God, you are so beautiful.

You take me there, drop me off, and leave me wanting you more.

I crawled into the bed and wrapped myself around him. When he got over his anger, he wrapped me in a tight, solid package against his soft, hot skin.

"I'm still crazy 'bout you," I mumbled under my breath.

He didn't reply.

He never did.

And I doubt he ever would.

I woke up close to four o'clock at the tail end of *Oprah*. She was remembering her spirit. Something I so desperately needed to do.

Sky was still holding me.

I kissed his forehead, slid out of the bed, gathered myself, and wiped the drool from the corners of my mouth.

"I'll call you later," I said.

"Okay."

I blew a kiss and exited quietly out the back door.

Weeks had gone by and I was well on my way to healing.

Lorenzo was a distant memory. Retrospect taught me that he wasn't the *last* man, because I had met so many more on the heels of his departure.

But I had a new attitude and a written contract between flesh and spirit to "keep my legs closed" because, unfortunately, they opened too easily. I posted the contract on my bathroom mirror because I needed a daily reminder.

Unfortunately, I was an expert on the theology of the one-night stand and the devastation it wreaks. The Japanese dealt with Hiroshima, the U.S. had to regroup after Pearl Harbor, but for me it was the aftermath of not keeping my legs closed. I was just beginning to get my swing back when the consistency of an inconsistent life paid me a visit.

Hunched on both knees I heaved my breakfast *again*.

I never threw up, so I didn't understand.

I didn't understand just long enough to check my calendar, count the days, and determine that I was four days late.

I had never been late a day in my life.

My first reaction was to flip out completely, but I had to keep it together so I could do some thinking.

Okay.

Thinking . . .

I'm thinking Lorenzo . . .

A dark night . . .

A horny woman . . .

A virile man . . .

Intercourse.

No condom.

Throwing up.

Nauseous.

Swollen breasts.

A bloated belly.

Four days late.

Hmmmm . . .

I'm thinking hysteria would be a viable option right now.

"I can't understand you when you're this hysterical!" Sky screamed.

I was on the bed.

Then the floor.

On the bed.

Then back to the floor.

"What's the matter?" he asked again, pulling me to him, locking me inside his embrace. And there I was. But where was I? Inside myself. Dying out loud. Spilling a lot of tears while my eyes rested under their own sleep deprivation.

"I'm in trouble, Sky," I whispered under shallow breath.

"What's wrong?" he asked, eyes wide with fear.

A pregnant pause passed before another word was said. How could I tell him the truth? How could I tell this man that I longed for so deeply and intensely that I was carrying someone *else's* baby?

How could I find the heart to tell him that I didn't really know my child's father? And how could I, with any self-respect attached to my being, mouth the words, "I don't even know his last name"?

Dear God.

I can tell you the size of his penis. I can also tell you where his birthmark is. I can tell you if he's got an innie or an outie belly button. I can tell you his butt is hairy. I can tell you how his face twists upon ejaculation and that his favorite position is doggy style. I can tell you he's a rather oral man, if you just have to know that, too. But please don't ask, please don't ask who he is, because I just couldn't tell you that.

"I'm pregnant . . ." the words rolled, stopped, then dropped, filling the room with heavy air. And while he adjusted to the news there was silence.

And embarrassment.

And uncertainty.

And that somber feeling that settles on heart attack victims just before they expire.

"How far along?" he asked.

"I don't know."

"Have you taken a pregnancy test?"

Test?

"No," I said shaking my head. "I hadn't thought about it. I'm four days late."

"Then how do you know for sure you're pregnant?"

"I feel it," I murmured. "My body's shifting . . . trust me . . . I can just feel it."

"Why don't we go to the drugstore and pick up a pregnancy test?" he suggested.

"No," I snapped.

"Why?"

"Because I don't want to know . . ."

"Wait, I thought you already *knew*?" he said.

"I do know, but I don't know."

"That doesn't make any sense," he said.

"I know, but it's not confirmed, and until it's confirmed it's not real, and if it's not real I don't have to do anything about it. Get it? Until there's a real problem I don't have to come up with a real solution."

"Oh, now that makes about as much sense as sleeping with a guy and not using a condom," he said sarcastically.

"You have awful timing," I said. "That was an awful thing to say to me right now."

"I know," he said apologetically, offering me an embrace. "I'm sorry."

I fumbled in the bathroom for what seemed an eternity trying to pee straight.

Not sideways.

Not at an angle.

Not too much, not too little.

I didn't want to spill or splash. I just wanted to spray a steady stream, directly on the goddamned strip so it could answer the heavy question looming over my existence.

If only one line appeared, it meant that God had given me a reprieve and spared me the agony of the rest of my life. But if two lines appeared, two little blood-red, strong, vibrant lines of condemnation, what would that mean?

It meant that my mother would lose her great parent upgrade and I would be an outcast. The church would declare Michael Morgan an official screwup and meddling women would gossip about me at their Sunday afternoon picnics.

You know Colleen's child was fornicating.

She was a big-time fornicator.

Mother would die a thousand deaths before turning her cheek to offer a deaf ear to loose lips.

I couldn't bear to stand in this tiny bathroom and wait on the pregnancy test to do its thing.

Three minutes.

Three mother-loving minutes, which by the way felt like a lifetime.

"Well?" Sky asked eagerly, pacing just outside the door.

Why was he *so* concerned? He acted as if he were the sperm donor on this project.

I opened the door and came out.

"Three minutes," I said.

We both sat on the edge of his bed in silence.

We waited two minutes and fifty-nine seconds before Sky got off the bed and did a slow grind toward the bathroom.

He walked.

I prayed.

Jesus, please let this be a menstrual misunderstanding, I begged.

Please let my eggs be off-schedule instead of fertilized. Please let my uterus post a no-vacancy sign to embryos today. Good Nelly. At this point all I could hope is that my uterus slipped out of my body and washed down the drain with last night's bathwater. Yes, please let me be uterus-less and if none of this feasible, then, God, please let me be sterile.

"You're pregnant," Sky confirmed from across the room as his eyes fixated on two red lines. "You're 99.99 percent pregnant," he added, as if I needed clarification of just how pregnant I could actually be.

Damn.

I was somebody else right now, but didn't know who. I was an innocent bystander watching the untold story of so-and-so, not me.

Her.

Not me.

The chick over there.

Not me.

The tramp on the edge of the bed who was a thousand miles overdue for an oil change and two weeks behind on a bikini wax.

Not me.

The former choirgirl turned slut.

That's her, not me, and this is her drama. This is her failed attempt at humanity, not my own. I was the therapist for the brokenhearted and bruised of spirit. I was the girl with the answers when the questions came at 180-degree angles dressed up in disguise. I am the poetically healed, innovative born-again believer for those perpetually down on their luck.

That's her, not me.

She's in a bad way, not *me*.

She's the one having a baby by a guy she just met, doesn't know, and will probably never meet again. She just lost her hope of being a childless bride. Now her wedding dress will have to include an extra thirteen inches around the waist. She couldn't catch her last dream because it boarded a fast-moving vehicle and disappeared into a foggy night.

The last thing she wanted to do was reproduce with a stranger.

The last thing she wanted to do was become a statistic.

The last thing she wanted to do was make a hard life *harder*.

That's *her,* not me, caught inside a situation behind four walls with no doors.

"What are we going to do?" asked Sky.

"This isn't your dance," I said.

"What can I do to help?" he insisted on asking.

"Marry me," I said. And if I thought there was a snowball's chance in hell that he would have accepted, I would have gotten down on one knee and waited for a reply. Instead, a kiss on the forehead by him would have to substitute for a lifelong commitment. I closed my eyes as his lips rested against the crinkle of my forehead. I closed them to make room for tears.

———

Once I settled under the shock and embarrassment of it all, I scurried across town to visit Mabel. Now, it wouldn't be right to talk about Mabel without a proper introduction.

Mabel was a fifty-seven-year-old woman with better-than-average vision. In fact, her sight was so acute she could see into the future.

Mabel wasn't your everyday run-of-the-mill fortune-teller. Oh, no, Mabel was a psychic with issues. For starters, she had a weight problem. She was so large that her weight exceeded the legal limit to fly on a single airline ticket. Mabel had to buy two tickets if she wanted to fly. But that wasn't a big deal, because Mabel didn't fly much after she lost her leg. The doctor cut it off. It wasn't a mistake that he took her leg, it was necessary. Diabetes exacted her limb because Mabel consistently forgot her insulin shots. I wondered if she remembered her shot when she woke up each morning to a heavy body that had to be toted around on one leg.

"Rub my leg," she said to me one time during a visit to her home shortly after the amputation. "Rub it . . . it hurts," she whined.

I touched her right leg and she hissed at me.

"Not that one!" she scowled. "It's the other leg that's hurting."

Mabel, you don't have another leg! They chopped it off, remember?! I wanted to scream. But I couldn't be that cold-blooded, so I let it go and pretended to rub a limb that wasn't there. As my hands stroked empty bedsheets, Mabel sighed with relief.

Mabel had one good eye and one lazy, drifting eye. She wore

her hair in matted dreadlocks. In truth, Mabel was evil. Not her heart, just her presentation. Raw around the edges. Most people were afraid of her and I understood. But that was because no one understood her gift of piercing the future with painful accuracy. If Mabel said it would happen, it was as good as done, and that scared most common folks to death. But it wasn't easy soliciting Mabel's cooperation because she was stingy with information.

Mabel didn't charge for her readings, but donations were mandatory. How contrary is that? But she didn't necessarily ask for cash. Sometimes she just wanted "goods" from her priority list, which included fine liquor in a bottle. But when my budget was crunched, malt liquor was an acceptable substitute. She was also partial to chicken wings, potato salad, nine-volt batteries for her vibrator, and Allen Iverson posters.

Go figure.

"What are you looking for today, Michael?" she asked under a heavy voice, sprawled backward in an oversized chair, clutching a cane for comfort and support.

I sat across from Mabel in the dark room choking on myrrh incense. I lowered my eyes on purpose. She didn't like people *looking* at her. It was a respect thing. You never looked at her. You glanced. Peeked. Took notes and acknowledged, but you never looked dead on. It would get you cussed out and thrown out.

I eased a bottle of Kentucky bourbon out of my purse and sat it on the table. And then I took a deep breath. Nervous, I guess. Mable was fickle sometimes and I didn't know if Kentucky bourbon would be acceptable. If she was on a chicken-wing-and-potato-salad kick this week, delivering Kentucky bourbon would get me cussed out and thrown out.

Mabel eyed the liquor, then seized it, burying it between her balloonlike breasts. Her most valued possessions were lowered down into that cleavage. I was careful not to stare and even more careful not to judge, because if Mabel thought for one second that I was judging her black ass, that, too, would get me cussed out and thrown out.

Mabel looked at me.

Then she looked through me.

"Why are you here today?" she asked.

I wanted to reply with, "You're the damn psychic . . . tell me." But delivery of a comment like that would only get me—*you know the drill*—cussed out, thrown out.

"Desperation," I responded with nervous laughter.

"Mmmm . . . desperation," nodded Mabel. "The devil's foundation that thing we call desperation. Why so desperate?" she asked, glaring at me with those ugly red eyes. It was enough to make me jump up out of my seat and run the hell out of her house. And had it not been for my authentic appreciation of her gift, I would have been gone.

Seriously.

Been gone.

"You have options," she said.

"Pardon?" I asked.

"Pardon yourself," she flared. "You sit in my house and pretend not to know what I'm talking about."

I wanted to object with the following, "Could your fat ass be a little more clear?" but you *know* where that would get me, right?

"That alone is enough to get you cussed out and thrown out," she reminded. "Pretending you don't know about the seed you're carrying."

Oh, that.

"Yes," I replied under shallow breath.

How could I possibly forget?

"The seed! The seed!" she shouted, clapping both hands together like a zoo monkey. "You know the seed!" she spat, spurt, and spouted. I never mentioned to Mabel that I was pregnant. And only a couple of weeks into the ordeal, there would be no way for her to know, but still she knew.

Sometimes I hated dealing with Mabel because she was stone nuts and could be abusive at times, but even though she was a temperamental loose cannon, I couldn't stay away from her nutty ass as long as she still beheld "the gift."

"Your baby's father is tangled up," she said as her red eyes drifted backward into her head. She closed her eyes and began to *see*. And this was the most fragile and uncertain time of my visit. Mabel was leaving to "go there," wherever it was that she went to gather data.

"Your baby's father is tangled with a newborn son."

Does that mean I'm carrying a boy? I wanted to ask, but dared not.

You were not allowed to speak when Mabel was speaking.

You were not allowed to ask questions. You were not allowed to interrupt for clarification. You were barely allowed the courtesy of your own breath.

All you could do was take the information, no matter how ludicrous, and tuck it under your belt. And eventually, every piece would find a place to fit. *Destiny* would see to that.

"There's an anchor tied around his foot. A heavy anchor," she said. Then she moaned and writhed in her chair before beginning to speak in a foreign tongue. Then she stopped, opened her eyes and looked at me.

"Good-bye," she said.

That's it? I wanted to blurt. That's all I get for a bottle of Kentucky bourbon and a twenty-dollar tip in cash. But I didn't dare complain because she would forbid me from returning.

I relinquished the twenty dollars and moved toward the front door.

"Michael," she called.

I stopped but didn't turn around.

"You want more answers, right?" she questioned.

I nodded.

"It would be a waste of my good conversation to give you answers that you already have within," she said.

"I just want to know what I should do," I said, filling up with tears.

"Call him," she said. "Call him up and spill your truths. You'll know where to go from there."

Cell phones have distinctive rings, I thought as the phone rang a second, then third time. I was hoping it would roll into voice mail and then I would be off the hook, no pun intended.

"This is Lorenzo," he answered in a brisk, hurried voice.

I froze.

"Hello?" he snapped impatiently.

"Lorenzo," I said with that voice. You know *that* voice? "Lorenzo?" I reaffirmed.

Silence.

He *knew* it was me.

"Hey," he said flatly, killing what was left of my spirits with his icy reception.

"It's Michael."

"Oh . . . yeah," he said, trying to play off disaffection. "Hey, what's up? I been meaning to call you, but I've been busy with this job and shit."

"Mmmmmm," I said, rolling my eyes.

"I been traveling, trying to make things happen. I'm trying to get out of this hole I'm in, you know what I'm saying," he said sounding more like an ass by the minute. "And you know, I got my entertainment business on the side. I'm a businessman by day, businessman by night. All this work leaves no time for Lorenzo to kick it like he used to. You get what I'm saying, baby? And that's the reason I haven't called. You get what I'm saying?"

"Listen, Lorenzo, why you haven't called me isn't a priority and the only reason I dug your number out of the trash was because I need to talk to you."

"So," he said with attitude. "What's up?"

"We need to sit down for a face-to-face."

"Like I said, I'm pretty busy."

"It's important," I reiterated, petitioning for cooperation without heavy coercion.

"I'll hit you back," he said, trying to rush me off the line.

"Lorenzo, this is serious," I said with a tone.

"What's up?" he asked even more agitated than before. "Like I said . . . I'm one busy brother . . ."

"Well," I paused to leash my temper, "can you put something on your calendar for me?"

"Depends. I've got a lot going on. You get what I'm saying?"

"Just make sure you leave a little room in your schedule for the D.A. That stands for the district attorney's office, because I'm sure in about nine months they're going to make a little time for you."

When I got there, he was waiting. It's amazing how a potential paternity suit can free up a busy man's entire afternoon. As I approached the restaurant's patio, I saw Lorenzo stationed behind a gang of shrubbery. *Cowards belong behind bushes*, I thought. He could disguise himself behind pretty leaves and plush moss, but he was still a poor excuse for a man as far as I was concerned.

The pinstripes on his suit caught my eye as I got closer. His navy suit was a show-stopper, and all the women on the patio were taking turns checking him out. I could see them offer final approval one by one, but they didn't know better. But I knew better and to know better meant to run like hell in the opposite direction from this big pretty man.

He got up when he saw me.

I wasn't impressed. It wasn't like he was giving me a standing ovation. He was probably searching for an emergency exit.

"How you doing?" he asked, extending a hand. And did I bother to accept? *I don't think so.* Instead, I sat across from him and stared into a pair of eyes that had sucked me in so deep at one time I couldn't even remember my name. But this time I wasn't searching for a soul mate, I was just searching for a *soul.*

"Sounds like we have business that needs to be taken care of," he said.

"I'm thirsty," I said ignoring his comment.

"Excuse me?" he asked looking at me baffled.

"I said I'm thirsty."

He motioned to the waitress, "Could we get some water?"

"Water?" I snapped.

His eyes danced between the waitress and me, and the two of them looked confused.

"Water," I told the waitress. "Bottled."

"Anything for you, sir?" the hotsy-totsy waitress addressed Lorenzo under subtle flirtation, which, by the way, wasn't so subtle at all.

"*Sir?*" I said harshly under my breath.

Once the path was clear Lorenzo leaned toward me and whispered in a low, cautious voice, "Are you bitter?"

"Bitter?" I asked loudly as puffs of white smoke seemed to seep from the top of my head.

This guy was oblivious.

"What would be my justification for being bitter?" I asked sarcastically.

He didn't say a word, just sat there with a blank expression.

"Do you know what really turns me on?" I asked stationed between sarcasm and insincerity. "Making love to a man and then never hearing from him again."

He didn't say anything and then I began imitating him, reminding him of the words he said to me that night. "I can be whatever you want me to be. What you need me to be," I repeated sarcastically.

Lorenzo tried to sink under the reflection of his shadow against the concrete wall. "Okay, okay, okay . . ." he said, fanning his hands. "Don't be so dramatic. I know you're pissed about me not calling back."

"Dramatic would be jumping over this table and slapping the shit out of you . . . don't tell me dramatic, goddamnit, I know dramatic when I see it." His eyes widened, lips silenced.

"I'm pregnant," I blurted. The couple sitting next to us shot eyes our way. Lorenzo shrunk but I didn't care. "What are we going to do about it?"

"We?" he asked, like he had never seen me before.

"*We*, Negro! Me and you!" I shouted.

"Lower your voice," he said becoming more conscious of awkward stares. Normally, I'm a soft-spoken black woman whose demeanor and presentation could pass for soulful Caucasian, but today had nothing in common with normal. And I was about half a second away from showing completely out.

"Okay," he said motioning to the waitress. "Jack Daniel's straight up," he said, loosening his collar. "We . . . We . . . are going to abort."

"*We* are going to discuss our options," I said.

"*We* have no options," he countered.

"There are alternatives," I defended.

"Not in my world," he said flatly.

"Why are you being so difficult, Lorenzo?"

"I'm not being difficult, I'm being real."

"Why won't you consider our options?" I begged.

"Options," he snickered. "There are no options, woman."

Woman? I've been reduced to an impersonal noun.

Woman?

"We don't even know each other," he went on to explain. "We're strangers, Michael."

"Well, if you would have called back . . ."

"I don't want this baby," he snapped. "Can't you get that through your thick skull? I don't *want* this kid!"

"Fuck you!" I snapped back.

"Fuck yourself," his only reply.

"Dickless wonder," I said resorting to juvenile behavior.

That was it. The older woman who sat adjacent to us choked on her latte.

"If you don't lower your voice, I will get up and walk out of here," he threatened. The waitress interrupted the flow by sitting my water down hard on the table.

"You can walk out of here and straight into hell, but that won't change blood to water or day to night. It is what it *is*,

Lorenzo. I'm pregnant. Don't you get it? Sex education is over. You've just graduated to the next level."

"How do you know it's mine?" was his only defense.

"How do you know it ain't?" was mine.

"You know what? You're right. I'll be the fall guy on this one," he shot back. He pushed away from the table, reached into his suit jacket, and pulled out a checkbook. "What's an abortion going for these days? A grand? Fifteen hundred?" he asked in a hurry.

I was so flabbergasted I couldn't even respond.

He tapped his pen against the table impatiently waiting for me to give him the magical number that could make it all disappear. Wave your checkbook in the air and bid farewell to bad vibrations. I was so disheartened by the insult that my eyes began to fill with water and I started to weaken. Anger, rage, and bitterness got in line behind hurt. And more hurt. "Lorenzo, is there any part of you that sees me as a human being?" I asked in a low voice.

He stopped and looked at me with a blank expression. I had feelings, but I doubt it ever occurred to him that I was human.

We're so opposite, the opposite sexes. We view them as men and they view us as women. Both sexes are so leery of what the other is bringing and leerier of what they're trying to take away. So much so that we forget that both sides are still human under our skin and issues, obsessions, dysfunction, and baggage.

"For one second will you just put down your checkbook and look at me? Remember that girl you made love to? The girl you held in your arms all night? The girl you promised . . ."

"Stop it, please. I can't," he interrupted. "Michael, I can't give you anything. I can't be there for you. I can't help you raise this baby. I can't participate in any of it."

"Why?" I asked. *Stupid fool that I was.*

"Because I'm married with a three-month-old son," he said under his breath.

Mabel's words cut through his own, *"He's tangled with a newborn son"* and *"An anchor tied around his feet."*

Snap.

London Bridge came falling down.

7

FRAGILE WINGS

Every time I parted the hair down the middle, her scalp crawled away.

"Crawling scalp," I said, throwing the comb down on the floor.

A scalp that crawls is a nightmare to deal with. The scalp moves because the skin is too lose on top of the head. Every time the hair is parted, the scalp shifts, making it impossible to get a straight part.

"Damn near impossible," I mumbled under short breath, shorter fuse. "Your scalp is crawling," I scolded my client. "Running around all over the place."

"Ooooohhh," said Timm dramatically.

Timm was my flamboyant associate and friend. There were days I adored him and equally the same number of days where I wished to gouge his eyes out. He was self-proclaimed bisexual, but I think he's full of crap. I believe he's totally gay, just doesn't have the guts to go all the way with it. He was half out of the closet, half in it. The half that was out of the closet was snappy and on-mark. The half that was in the closet hid behind cardigan and winter fleece.

Timm's feminine characteristics were dominant, but he was sprinkled with a hint of masculinity. So minor in comparison, his manhood was only detectable through the giant bulge midway between his waist and his knees. His eyes were big and oval, his lashes curly. His lips perked in the middle and his cheeks slid in and upward. His head reminded me of a skyscraper, the Sears Tower to be more precise.

Timm overdramatized *everything*. He was a walking, breathing public display. Every time a new client came in through the front door he buckled at the knees. There was gnashing of teeth and weeping that went on for way too long. I never knew why he carried on so. The deceased kept us eternally employed until the time when we would be called upon to join them, and to make a big deal over their passing was simply a giant waste of energy.

"Life lost in the height of its promise," he continued with his own patented version of madness, crying over Jeannette Cooper's corpse.

"She was ninety-seven years old," I said standing over Mrs. Cooper's body, looking cockeyed at Timm.

"If she could have just held on," he said adamantly.

"Held on for what? Her husband died six years ago, her daughter three years ago, and her son last year. She was rotting in an old age home that reeked of BenGay. What's the point?"

Timm threw both hands on his hips.

"Backgammon!" he said as if I didn't know. "Every Tuesday and Thursday, Mrs. Cooper played backgammon in the game room."

"So?" I said, dropping to the floor trying to find the comb.

"So?" he said, twisting his neck a little too far to the left.

"Yeah, so what?" I challenged.

"She *lived* for the game. Backgammon was her soul food. That's why she lived so long."

"How do you know all this trivia about dead people?"

"Catch 'em on a good day, like when they were living, and you'd be surprised what a dead man knows."

"Oh," I said, off in another dimension. I didn't have time for Timm and his dead people drama today. Hell, I had my own problems and from where I was standing, kneeling, bending, or leaning, Mrs. Cooper's issues were over.

"But anyway, girl, glad that's your head and not mine," said Timm, switching gears. "I am not in the mood for crawling scalp today."

He was so dramatic: distraught one minute, jubilant the next. He threw his body over the side of a chair and performed his usual "Dead Man Dying" routine by grabbing his throat, clutching his chest. It was pathetic, but funny, so I laughed.

I *needed* to laugh.

When Timm left to go harass the embalmers, I glanced at Mrs. Cooper. She looked so peaceful, like she was trying to smile on the heels of her last breath. She was either happy to be leaving "here" or ecstatic to be going "there." Either way she looked more content dead at ninety-seven than I did living at twenty-nine.

When was the last time I smiled like that? I asked myself. When was the last time I closed my eyes and smiled without expecting this, expecting that? When was the last time I actually sucked up a day's worth of air without trying to fill in all the gaps in between? Dear God it had been so long since my lungs were free to inhale and exhale without baggage and labored respiration. Most of my struggles centered around the journey for Band-Aids to heal undisclosed wounds precarious in nature.

I stood there for a while staring at Mrs. Cooper.

She wasn't plotting and scheming, manipulating and contemplating. She wasn't searching for perfection. She wasn't trying to stay one step ahead of the pain. Even after her husband died, Mrs. Cooper still kept a lover by her side—backgammon. Timm was right, it was her soul food. Backgammon wasn't my favorite activity in the world, but then again, who was I to say that the circular vanilla and chocolate chips had no value as they scurried across a velvet floor on an oddly designed board?

Shoot.

Who was I fooling?

I don't know what Mrs. Cooper's issues were and seeing as how she was dead, I can't exactly conduct a one-on-one with her. She could have very well been a cantankerous old bitch with spine curvature and hemorrhoids. She could have been the epitome of upright, misery on a cane, and backgammon could have been her disguise. A simple, but brilliant scheme indeed to conduct afternoon backgammon sessions while she and the old geezers devised plots to overthrow the nation, or should I say their nation, Shady Days Rest Home.

"Shame on you, Mrs. Cooper," I said aloud as I manipulated loose skin on her scalp to keep the parts straight.

"You're so lonely for breathing people, aren't you girl-friend?" said Timm, reentering as quickly as he had exited. *Sigh* from the narrator. He truly was a thorn in my buttocks.

"What do I have to do to get you to come out with me and my friends?" he asked.

"Kidnap me at gunpoint," I said without missing a beat.

"Oh, I forgot, you're *so* sophisticated," he said with a hiss.

Did he just hiss at me?

"It's not that."

"Then what is it?"

"I don't fit in, Timm. Your friends are all gay and we have nothing in common, except a mutual attachment to dick."

"Well, that's a start."

"No thanks," I mumbled under my breath.

"Beats being lonely."

"Who said I was lonely?" I asked defensively.

"Who said you weren't?" he asked, patting me on the back like my name was Lassie.

"Okay, there you go, starting shit," I said. "I'm not in the mood today, Timm."

"Your eggs are dying, girlfriend," he warned.

"My eggs are dying?" I repeated in disbelief.

"You better get over yourself and make a move to change your situation lest you die alone," he concluded. "You've lost thousands of eggs over your lifetime, ya know?"

"Well," I said packing up my curling irons and blow dryer. "Thank you for the scientific summation on the condition of my eggs. It just seems like a great travesty that you haven't been assigned to live my life, seeing as how you're such an expert on it."

Once the brilliant Timm realized that he *may* have offended me, he felt the need to compensate for his stupidity by saying, "No hard feelings though, right?"

"None taken," I replied halfheartedly, glancing at Lorenzo's two-thousand-dollar check. *Two grand can make babies disappear. Don't you know that by now?* My eyes were heavy staring at the check and so was my heart. "Timm, your level of retardation is much too high for me to ever take anything you say remotely serious,"

"I still love you girl," he said in jest, then disappeared again. *Thank God.* I turned my attention back to Mrs. Cooper's dead body. "Life always rips my fragile wings to death," I whispered. And that's how I felt at the moment.

Ripped.

And torn.

With child.

Without a soul.

I felt so inhumane, so unlike human.

And it just wasn't right, the situation and my life. I was

beginning to feel as I had always felt—like someone *stole* my happy ending, again.

I threw down my comb, walked out the door, and didn't look back. At least not that day.

8

SORRY

S
O
R
R
Y

His words fell like that.

"*Sorry.*"

Sorry what?

Sorry I came inside. Sorry I got you pregnant. Sorry I can't be there for this inconvenience. Sorry I was married and so sorry I didn't tell you that before I slipped inside you and planted a seed.

Sorry I'm just a player. Sorry I'm not for keeps. Sorry I have an integrity issue, and so sorry that I have such an obsession for women giving it up to strangers.

Sorry I can't take you to the clinic. Sorry I can't pick you up. Sorry I can't hold your hand when they lasso you up on top of the table. Sorry they'll put you under to bring you down and dig you out. Sorry they'll wash our seed down a disinfectant drain. Splish splash, a uterine bath.

Sorry.

Sorry.

Sorry.

Sorry it's your body. I wish it were mine instead, but I am the recipient of the penis and as such I am lacking the basic internal hookup to understand exactly what it is that you are going through. Perhaps if I were more in touch with my feminine side, I would understand the nature of the many tears you have spilled out onto your bathroom floor. But since we both know that's not plausible, the best I can do is pull out my checkbook and scribble the blues away. Can we scribble the blues away to the tune of two grand? That's a two followed by three zeros. Is that good enough? Two grand, a giant hug, and a parting smile. Isn't that good enough?

Sorry.

Sorry.

Sorry.

I stared at the check so hard the letters had started to bleed. He wrote the check from his business account to keep his wife from asking, "Excuse me darling, but who is Michael Morgan and why are you giving *him* two thousand dollars?"

He wrote the check from that account to save himself from the inevitable answer/the eventual truth. "Oh, Michael. Michael is a chick that I met one night at the 7-Eleven. I drove by her house, hit it, stayed all night . . . remember that night I told you I was negotiating a deal in Toledo? Yeah, that's right, dear. Remember that night? Well, that night I was knee deep in another woman's stuff, but that's no reason to be upset. It's not like I ever saw or called her again after that. It was just a sex thing and to make a long story short, the chick got pregnant and she's putting it on me. Of course the ho probably slept with every John Doe in town, but I forgot my condom so I can't be totally sure it ain't mine. Sorry for rambling baby, but the bottom line is the two grand is to take care of the problem, you know? Anyway, it's done, taken care of . . . baby . . . please put the gun away baby . . . put the gun away . . . it ain't that serious."

I could hear a crystal clear audio of their conversation in my head even though I knew he and his wife would never converse about Michael Morgan and her protruding uterus.

I wanted to rip the check to shreds and watch the tiny pieces sway in the wind and fall toward the ground. I had wished the check to be Lorenzo's heart and soul. And I wanted them to tear and bleed just like mine had done.

"What time is your appointment?" asked Sky, who was gently rubbing my shoulders as I lay my head in his lap, and he slowly brought me back to a reality that I needed to escape. I had come to his apartment to watch the game and take my mind off things. I had come to his door seeking distraction, or maybe I had come seeking deliverance.

"At 9 A.M.," I said, responding to his question without emotion.

"Are you okay with your decision?" he asked.

"How could anybody be okay with that decision?" I snapped.

"Then don't do it," he said.

I spun around to face him. He looked at me with big pretty eyes that were filled with great compassion. I wanted him to tell me that he loved me and say that he always had. I wanted him to drop to one knee and spring a diamond on me like they did in the movies. I didn't care if it was real or a cubic zirconia. Hell, I didn't care if he retrieved it from a box of Cracker Jacks. I just wanted it to be real—not the ring, just his intentions. I so desperately wanted him to say that this was our child, even though we'd never had intercourse.

"Don't do it if you're not sure, Michael," he said again.

"Do it with me?" I asked, not said. Asked, not begged. Just asked.

He pulled away, and that was my answer.

"Sorry," I said, feeling like a fool, standing in the backdraft of anger. I had liked this man for so long, why couldn't he give me *something* back? It wasn't fair to like someone so hard without a return. It was cruel for him not to like me back. So cruel.

"Why can't we be together, Sky? Why?"

"Because I don't feel what you feel," he said softly.

"Then tell me what you feel?" I asked. "*Show* me what you feel," I pleaded, touching the center of his chest with my hand.

Gee, nothing like the truth to topple you over the bitter edge.

"I can't show you something that doesn't exist," he said.

I could have rolled off the couch and smashed into the hardwood floor, headfirst, when he said that, but I was trying to save myself from greater complications like brain damage or humiliation.

Silence.

And then there was more silence.

And then, oh yeah, here they come . . .

I had been awaiting their arrival for a while now.

Tears.

Tears.

And more tears.

He tried to hold me but I rejected his embrace because sympathy was so damn insulting. I walked out of his house and slammed the door so hard that one of his wall paintings slammed to the ground.

Morning seemed an eternity away and still it rose without warning. I lay on my back counting sheep and dead babies, but I lost count when the phone rang.

Six A.M.? I reached for the phone with urgency. Six A.M. calls usually brought despair on the opposite end.

"Hello?" I said, trying not to sound like I hadn't slept in three days.

"Michael?" the deep voice crooned.

I knew who it was.

"I just wanted you to know that I'll be thinking about you today," he said.

I didn't respond.

"I wish I could be there for you," he added.

Still I didn't respond.

"I'm not an asshole or anything, even though you probably think poorly of me . . ."

"Lorenzo, please," I said.

"Okay . . . okay . . . I just wanted you to know that you're not alone in this."

I didn't respond at first, but then words came from where silence once was. "Lorenzo, in three hours I'll walk into an abortion clinic by myself and destroy a life that we created together. By the time you and the boys are having lunch, I'll be cramping and bleeding. By the time you make it home tonight to play with your son, I'll be here, not much different than I am right now, except of course that I'll be a baby killer. Around the time you and your wife are making love, I'll be on my knees pleading insanity to a God that I hope someday can forgive me. Lorenzo, it may not happen today and for the moment it appears you have escaped your eventuality, but one day when you least expect it, life will pay you back for your part in what happened between us." And then I disconnected.

Nine A.M. dropped like an eighteenth-century guillotine.

Sky drove me to the clinic just as we had planned the day before. The ride was ride was long and quiet.

My arrival at the facility was sobering. It was a surreal experience void of conscience. The initial stage of paperwork was overwhelming, but I had no choice but to rise to the occasion. I found it necessary to remove myself from the situation at hand, at least on an emotional level. My body had to stay and this I was sure of, but the rest of me had been cleared for departure.

There would be no time for whimpering because there were plenty of rights to waive. Should this, that, or the other happen, all privileges to sue had to be signed away.

I didn't have time to consider God and his commandments because I wouldn't stay here if I thought about it too hard. And truth of the matter, I was too preoccupied by what I was doing to reflect on what I was *doing*.

"Sign here, here, and here," said the woman in white.

I did as I was told without emotion. Why make a theatrical production out of it? What would a display of drama do for me now? Smudge my mascara and tempt my nose into running.

"Did you read it?" she asked. "You really should read it before you sign."

"I caught the highlights," I said, removed from it all.

"First time?" she asked bending toward a smile.

"People come back more than once?"

Her eyes dropped. I guess she saw this every day, the faint of heart entering the premises searching for a miracle. This was her reality. She was practically numb to the women with little pouches who came in seeking modern-day medicine to deflate their bellies, dilute their offspring, and wash them down an invisible drain. They fix the problem by denying it ever existed.

I offered a smile to the woman in white—a slight, awkward smile. I felt as sorry for her as she felt for me. I would assume it would be difficult to turn yourself off and pretend to offer the world a valuable service in the form of population control.

"Come with me," she said as I followed her down the long, sterile hall.

They took blood. It was standard procedure before exacting the patient's soul, I guess. This was followed by an ultrasound performed by a nurse who had left her personality at home. Following the ultrasound, I was sent to a holding room where other desperadoes waited for "their turn."

"Hell of a business," I said to another pregnant woman who just didn't want to be. *Oh God*, I thought. *What have you done this time, Michael Morgan? Just what the hell have you done?*

My mother would die if she knew.

Papa would die if he knew.

I would die if I knew.

My name was called like roll call in a kindergarten class, but the serious business of abortion was no child's play. I was introduced to a tiny little white room with an examination table, a pair of stainless-steel stirrups, and a bottle of disinfectant spray to drown out the odor of falling fetuses.

"Remove your clothing, put this on, and lie on the table," directed another personality-less human being who pointed me in the direction of a paper gown. There's no feeling that can quite describe the sensation of slipping into an oversized paper towel. Harsh perhaps?

Several minutes later a male doctor entered. *A man got me in this predicament and a man will get me out.* The irony evoked laughter. The doctor glanced at me in confusion. He slipped into his gloves as I conformed to the proper position.

"Scoot down farther," he said. "Farther," he said again.

Farther.

And farther.

Till my butt cheeks nearly clapped together at the edge of the table.

"Okay. Good," he said.

"How many of these do you do a day?" I asked.

He offered no answer.

I laughed again. A laugh whose source was pain, but the doctor didn't know that. I could tell the doctor was uncomfortable and was probably pondering my stability. And I laughed again because there he was, standing at the edge of my vagina, peeking in. But the good doctor owned a penis and would never know, even on his worst day, how it would feel to switch places, lie on his back, and assume the position.

The drug man entered and found a vein.

"Count to ten," he said.

"Sorry," was all I managed to say before I even made it to one.

9

THE WRONG SUIT

Mrs. Cooper's part stayed straight and her memorial service played out beautifully. Timm never convinced me to barhop with the homosexuals, and Sky and I ascended beyond our last awkward conversation about why we couldn't be together. Lorenzo never called again, and eventually the blood dried up and I did extra penance for time spent at an abortion clinic.

I also signed on for birth control pills because they work a hell of a lot better than chance.

I asked God for forgiveness and deep down inside I tried to prepare myself for hell, just in case, because dead people don't like surprises. I convinced myself that I had done the right thing despite painful groin kicks from morality.

No I hadn't done the *right thing*, but I was convinced I'd done the *best* thing and that was the only way I could rock myself to sleep at night. And then I split in two, disconnected myself from what I had done. The moment the procedure was over, it immediately became part of my *past*. And that's how I managed to go on, without hating myself entirely for what I'd done.

"And the beat goes on," I whispered to Sky at the dinner table. I ventured to my mother's house once a month to have dinner with her, and lately I had been bringing Sky because my life resembled normal with a strong, steady man by my side.

My mother thought we were the perfect little couple, so perfect in fact that she didn't understand why we had not yet married.

I had only known him six months.

Come on now.

Mother could read my heart and knew that I had fallen for Sky, but what she couldn't see was that my beautiful breasts and sensuous curves did not appear to be enough for him.

"He's such a pretty man," said Mother, glowing as we cleared the table. "Have you seen his jaw structure?" she asked.

"Jaw structure?" I asked, face twisted.

"It's perfect," she boasted. "I can't believe you haven't noticed."

Hhhhhmmmmm. Jaw structure? I was more in tune to things like job stability, education, and sexual preference. But maybe I was on the wrong boat. Maybe I should have reevaluated my criteria and reduced it to something simple like jaw structure.

"No, Mother. I haven't noticed," I said.

Mother gave me one of those looks. The "I can see all of the stuff you're hiding behind" look. I looked away because I didn't want her to look inside my soul and see bitterness and sadness. I didn't want her to look just beyond the exterior and see all the broken hearts, floating demons, and shipwrecked dreams.

"You need to come with me to church on Sunday," she suggested.

"Thank you for dinner, Mrs. Morgan," said Sky interrupting as he embraced my mother, rescuing me from a dishonorable reply just in the nick of time.

"It's always a pleasure," she said with a smile. When I glanced at her, she winked and whispered in my left ear, "Don't forget to check out the jaw line."

The ride home with Sky felt nice. It always did as we curved through winding roads, playing hide-and-seek with Mother Nature. One beautiful bronze man behind the wheel of a sports car cutting through boundless highway with a babe to his right. Shakespeare couldn't even write prose that pretty.

I reached for his hand and held on. And to my surprise he reciprocated and held my hand back, which only made my heart skip two, maybe three beats. I closed my eyes and enjoyed the ride. I even engaged in a hallucination or two, dreaming that Sky made love to me all night long, without even stopping for water. And I moaned.

"What are you thinking about?" he asked with slight suspicion.

"You," I said.

He smiled.

"So what are you thinking about?" he asked.

"Don't tempt me," was my only reply.

"Why? I really want to know. What are you thinking about?"

"About being with you," I said with caution.

"You are with me," he said, squeezing my hand.

"No. I mean *being* with you."

"You mean being with me, physically?" I couldn't believe he was going there. *Why was he going there?*

"Yes," I admitted sheepishly. "Being with you physically."

He smiled, then nodded, which only began to make me crazy because now I desperately wanted to know what *he* was thinking about.

"What?" I blurted out so quickly I nearly cut off my oxygen supply.

"Nothing." He shook it off.

"No, you can't leave me hanging like that! What?"

He laughed out loud as his eyes rolled back into his head.

"What if I said okay?"

I let go of his hand, sat upright, and looked into his eyes. "Okay to sex??" I asked flabbergasted.

"Yeah, what if I said okay to sex?"

"With me?" I had to throw in for clarification.

"Who else?" he asked, annoyed.

I coughed. No, I think I choked. No, I think I slid out on the floor and fell face forward on the floor mat.

"But I thought you didn't see me in that light?" I tossed out for discussion.

He looked at me and I at him and neither of us said a word.

"Are you?" I asked, horrified that he might actually answer.

"Am I what?" he asked, which led me to believe we were in big trouble if he was waiting on me to answer his heart.

"Attracted to me?" I pushed to know.

He didn't answer and he never would. Instead he would shut himself down and allow ambiguity to lead the dance. And that was the end of that conversation, but as quickly as one complex interaction dissipated, another one quickly emerged in its place. So what the hell?

By the time we arrived home I could already feel the angst of a night that I was uncertain I was ready to let go. I sat in the car after he had turned off the engine and stared at the moon. He sat there, too, staring upward toward the sky. Both of us seemed to be making our own personal wishes on stars too far for reaching.

"You ready?" he asked disrupting the flow.

"Ready for what?" I said, looking into his eyes.

Ready for this beautiful night to end? Ready to creep into a lonely bedroom and reenter a life of longing and loneliness. No thanks. I wanted to pass on that brilliant opportunity, so I motioned for him to go without me.

His eyes cut through me. He seductively took me by the hand and led the way.

And I followed.

To the platform bed, where he unbuttoned his cotton shirt and slowly directed my hand to the dents of his chest. I touched him and, "Oooohhhhh," I moaned aloud and looked away, frightened to look him in the eyes for fear this might be another fantasy that felt too real.

He bent his body toward me so I could feel him better.

"Ooooohhhh," I moaned, because I couldn't help myself. Months of make-believe were on the verge of coming true as I eased my hand over his hard nipples, slightly teasing them with my touch.

He slightly moaned as he looked into my eyes.

I felt my face flush as I leaned into his chest and sucked his nipples like a newborn seeking sustenance. I could feel his heartbeat, a steady, gushing sound heightened by labored breathing, his and mine, mine and his, his and mine.

"Again. Again," the words swelled from his throat. "Again."

I followed the direction of his body hair against my tongue as it swirled below the pores of his skin. I wanted to take his lips and hold them hostage. I ached to slip my tongue inside his mouth and swallow his teeth, his tongue, sweat, and secretions.

I came up for a kiss but as I went for his lips, he turned away. I searched for lips again and again he turned away. I scanned his face to the other side and a cruel dance ensued, me searching for his lips and finding them gone, searching for lips, finding them gone. I didn't want a full-scale production with lights, a crowd and budget, I just wanted some lips, his lips to be precise, pressed against mine. And if he wanted to toss in a bonus, throw in some tongue, I might just collapse onto the floor. If I could get all of that right now, without begging, pleading, and foaming at the mouth, I would die for it. And I would be willing to die and wait for his lips to resuscitate and reincarnate me, but he just kept turning away.

"I want to kiss you," I said barely breathing or perhaps breathing too much. "And I want you to kiss me back."

He stood tall, pushing me low and lower till I was on my knees caressing his erection. I scanned his manhood, up and down, down and up. It was hot, large, and erect, curled upward with a single vein throbbing due north.

"Ooooohhhh," he moaned as I licked the extremities.

He groaned. It sounded good and appeared normal, but it lacked sensuality and felt weird. And this is where I began to doubt his sexuality. He seemed like a novice at it, scanning my female body. Honestly, I couldn't be certain if he had ever seen a vagina, much less felt one with his own bare hands. Something felt bizarre or off. It didn't feel right, didn't feel natural. *Is he wearing the right suit?* I thought. Was he wearing a full heterosexual suit with all the proper gear and instructions? He's touching me, but I can't *feel* him. He's rubbing me, but *where*? He's definitely a man with all the right man parts, but how are they all connected? Are the wires running the right way and are they supposed to intersect like this?

I spent years waiting for the connector flight and now I'm finally riding it. I am thirty-five thousand feet above sea level, but still chained to soil and ground. How could that be? Am "I" in the right suit? This paradigm clouded my thoughts as he gently laid me down and relieved my clothing of its duties.

He stared at my womanhood like this was the first time he had ever been in the presence of a naked woman. And as his hands ventured the depth of erotica, it felt more like he was searching for my sexual compass rather than seeking to give me pleasure.

I didn't moan, just looked away. But I think he wanted me to moan.

"Your body is," he said grasping for words, "is . . ." he fumbled and mumbled, "is . . ."

Why are you distracting me from the orgasm I am trying to have? I wanted to protest. I can't come *and* help you fill in the blank at the same time. Suddenly, his touch was a source of aggravation. Months and months of waiting and *this* is all I get? He climbed on top but didn't fit. He was heavy against me, awkwardly seeking entry, he was a stranger to my kingdom.

Once inside, a crazy ride began. He was pushing and shoving trying to make his circle fit inside my square. It was devoid of beat and rhythm. How could he make love to me like this? "Use your hips," I wanted to instruct. "Arch your back and find your thrust. Don't get on top of me and bounce! Were you absent the day school offered sex education?"

Before I could work up a sweat or a decent amount of anger and resentment, he came. And even his orgasm could be critiqued. I thought orgasm was supposed to be the climax, but his was more like an interruption of the regular broadcast. There was nothing climactic about it at all, other than the fact that he stopped. It wasn't the explosive eruption that I was accustomed to witnessing. I was waiting for his eyes to roll back into his head and his face to twist and contort. I wanted the vein to bulge in the middle of his forehead and his mouth to open involuntarily and drool to leak. If he wouldn't have stopped and quickly dismounted, I wouldn't have even had to ask, "Did you come?"

"Yes," he said unaffected. Okay, perhaps this is where I should insert these two words: *courtesy lay*.

Courtesy lay from a guy wearing the wrong suit.

10

MORNING

Morning comes without fail and that's the bitch of it all. It rises out of nowhere, trickily hidden in the britches of night. It creeps against the crack of darkness, hanging skeletons out for public display. But that's not the gripe I have with morning. The gripe I have with morning is simple. It ascends without regard for my personal shame offering way too much attention on all the embarrassing stuff that was done the night before.

And so there I was with Sky. It was an awkward moment at best. I didn't look his way nor did he look mine. We both thought it wise to maintain our pretend distance. And even though it was no secret that just hours ago his penis had been inside of me, I think we chose to ignore it until we were better equipped to handle the aftermath of a night that never should have happened. It was time to face the mo' better blues: the guy just *wasn't* into me. I didn't know what his story was, but I presumed it could have been any number of issues such as:

LACK OF LIBIDO.
SEXUAL PERFORMANCE ANXIETY.
TECHNICAL DIFFICULTIES.

We tried to overlook everything from the intercourse to the stale odor of day-old sex floating around. Actually, Sky didn't overlook that because the first thing he did upon waking was open a window. Dry semen stains were not a topic for discussion so we filled in communication gaps with irrelevant conversation.

"Sleep good?" he asked.

"Yeah," I said, trying to pretend that I wasn't trying to pretend.

"You want breakfast?" he offered.

I smiled. It was nice to know that he didn't just want me for my beautiful body, which by the way I don't think he noticed at all, and that only messed with my head.

"Sure," I responded.

When he stood up he had a throbbing erection.

"How do you like your eggs?"

"Hard," I said. "No pun intended," I added, glancing at his erection. And to this his only reply, "Toast?"

"Okay."

"Wheat or sourdough?"

"Wheat," I confirmed under the pressure of his beautiful body and my tardy orgasm that didn't show up the night before.

"How do you like your coffee?" he asked.

"Brown like you," I said smiling.

"Okay," he said dryly.

I must be in the twilight zone. He's beautiful, buff, intelligent, sexy, charming, and naked. And I'm beautiful, fit, intelligent, sexy, charming, *and* naked, too.

He's hard.

I'm wet.

It fits.

The pieces work, but they're all disconnected. He's acting more like a waiter offering the breakfast special at Denny's than a man wanting a little morning nooky. What's going on here? Perhaps his erection was a reflex and not a basic instinct that draws him to my sexuality. At this point I had no other choice but to assume what every woman assumes about a man she cannot pull in with the strange fruit that sits between her legs.

He must be gay.

"Are you? . . ." I stopped.

And he paused from his journey to the kitchen and turned to face me.

"What?" he asked.

"Are you? . . ." I couldn't get it out, spit it out.

"What's up Michael?" he asked torn between curiosity and aggravation.

"Are you? . . ."

Gay, I wanted to scream.

Gay, I wanted to fall out on the floor on all fours, both hands, both feet. Gay, I was dying to know. How could he not tell me? How could he make me come right out and be rude enough to ask? How could he not volunteer? How could he not carry a membership card? Why couldn't he just slap his sexual identity on the back of his driver's license or social security card and save both of us the humiliation? He could save me the humiliation of asking and him the stress of answering.

"Okay?" I asked. "Are you okay?"

"Fine," he said like it was no big deal. "Are you okay?" he asked, turning the tables, staring at me like a human oddity.

"Good," I said feeling a wind of embarrassment.

My nipples were so hard. *Oh Lord.* Please don't let him mistake these headlights as a sign of sexual arousal. And he didn't. He just turned and walked into the kitchen where he started whistling "Take Me Out to the Ballgame."

"Great," I mumbled sarcastically under my breath. I stepped into his shower, turned on the water, and did a thorough exam of all of the parts of my body that were supposed to feel good last night. *Yes,* they were still there. Why didn't they show up last night?

"Yes, yes," I accidentally moaned.

Rubbing.

Caressing.

Fondling.

Masturbating.

Manipulating my breasts and secret places in the Magic Kingdom. I was really getting into this vibe and could have gone all the way with it, if I hadn't locked eyes with Sky who was standing on the other side of the cracked shower curtain staring at me. He was holding a fresh towel in one hand and a bad opinion of me in the other. Okay, I was the last freak on earth. Need I say all activity ceased? He sat the towel down on the sink and exited without incident. I immediately dissolved into a 130-pound blob of brown skin and slithered down the shower drain. And that . . . that was my morning.

11

CHEMISTRY

After I left Sky's house I went directly to Mabel's because I needed some psychic understanding of what was really going on. And of course I needed a twenty-dollar bill, a bucket of greasy chicken wings, and a bottle of respectable liquor.

Prior to gaining access into her apartment, I endured the usual brutality. External interrogation by blood-red eyes that cut my frame head to toe, indecipherable gibberish and unjustified paranoia, which could only be satisfied by a partial strip search. Once I was cleared for entry, Mabel hobbled one step backward and I was allowed inside. But those scarlet eyes followed every step I took toward a giant black chair in the center of an empty room where the readings were done.

Once I relinquished the goods, Mabel shoved the liquor under the couch and the twenty-dollar bill under her left breast. It was all enough to traumatize me for life, but I had to move beyond it. She then proceeded to inspect the chicken wings for quality and authenticity, I guess. Once her giant greasy lips surrendered to the carnage, we were ready to begin. Or so I thought.

"Toothpicks?" she asked.

"Toothpicks?" I repeated.

"Where are the toothpicks?" she snapped.

"Uh . . . well . . . um . . . I don't have any . . ." I stuttered and tripped over the words. "Toothpicks."

"How could you bring tough chicken wings with no toothpicks?"

"I didn't think about it . . ."

"Next time you *must* bring toothpicks or there will be no reading!" She practically spit on me. "You *must* bring toothpicks! Write that shit down . . . toothpicks."

I'll tell you what I wanted to write down—a note to myself to buy a lead brick and bash her in the head with it, but that would no more happen than my arrival at her doorstep with a box of toothpicks. And Mabel's fat ass would just have to deal with that. She was running the show, but she also had to remember that if there were no pawns to play with there would be no show to run. So the hefty heifer couldn't get too carried away with her demands.

She began the session with a deep moan, which frightened me because she normally didn't start off moaning.

"Gas," she said with a bitter smile.

Traumatized for life, I tell you—that's what I'm going to be when this is all said and done—traumatized for life.

After several minutes, Mabel still hadn't said a word. I stared at the walls and she closed her eyes, allowing both of us to sit in excruciating silence. I continued to wait patiently until I heard the buzzing sound of a greedy chicken wing–eating psychic who had gone to sleep and begun to snore.

That's it!

I jumped from my seat careful not to wake Sleeping Beauty and did a mad dash toward the door.

That's it, Mabel!

There will be no more chicken wings and potato salad!

No more Colt 45!

No more nine-volt batteries!

And forget about ever seeing a box of toothpicks!

"That's it!" I promised under hushed breath. I dare not insult her lest she erect a voodoo doll and prick me to death with stick pins and chicken gristle.

As my hand turned the knob, I was interrupted by the sound of a groggy old woman with a gift, "Leave him alone, Michael. He's laying with the devil."

I know I'm not supposed to make eye contact with Mabel, nor am I supposed to ask questions, but I spun around, looked her dead in the face, and said, "What?"

"Good-bye," was her only reply.

And good-bye meant just that.

Good-bye.

Reading over.

To push Mabel beyond what she was willing to give equated to self-destruction. Mabel operated on a piece-by-piece basis. She never gave a lot of information, just enough to tangle you in mysterious truth and ensure she would be fed again tomorrow.

There would be no more insights today, so I took her words, short in length, long in meaning, tucked them under my belt, and left.

I knocked on the pale green door with unsteady nerves. I didn't know what to expect on the other side of this splintered wood door. Molly Wood was finally out of rehab and trying to get her life together under the watchful eye of the Chateau Paradise halfway house. But when I found the clustered apartment unit, it was anything but Paradise.

The slovenly high-rise had a crook in its back and a corn on its baby toe. With a cockroach infestation and ugly on every corner, the only thing missing was the city's official welcome sign, "Welcome to Shitville, USA. Now Get the Hell Out."

I tried to disguise my angst about the neighborhood, the people, the graffiti, the planes flying low and crack addicts flying high because I didn't want my best girlfriend to think I was tripping off the scenery. But you know what? I was tripping off the scenery.

Knock, knock, knock.

No answer.

Knock, knock, harder.

Still no answer.

"I'll be damned," I cursed, reaching into my purse to verify the address. "I knew she wouldn't be living in a place like this." But before I could confirm an error had been made, the door spun open, almost tearing from its hinges, "Babeeeeeeeee!"

howled Molly as she wrapped herself around me, smothering my face with biscuit-and-gravy-style kisses.

"I missed you, baby. Missed you so much!" she said again and again, till the repetition beat me down.

"I missed you, too," I said soaking her up.

"You okay?" I asked, scanning the room searching for a reason to put on my bulletproof vest. The place was a dump. I had to do the two-step around a tribe of roaches just to gain access into the joint.

"I'm good, baby . . . real good," she said trying to convince me. But I knew the real deal because my mother hadn't raised a fool. If she were so good she wouldn't be courting cocaine on a consistent basis, destroying everything she was trying so hard to save.

I loved Molly Wood, but every time I turned around she was confirming the necessity of a twelve-step program. But I didn't judge her because I had not found within myself confirmation that I was any better.

"Where are we going today, baby?" Molly asked like a wide-eyed child. She was excited about today as I had promised her this would be a "day worth remembering."

"Never mind," I said. "Just make sure you're wearing comfortable walking shoes."

"Can I wear these?" she asked pointing to her five-inch, leopardlike spike heels. Molly always had to be so damn flamboyant from the tip of her breasts to the ends of her bleached-blonde hair. I referred to her as "Queen of the Unordinary" because nothing about her was simple *or* ordinary. And just for the record, words like *simple* and *ordinary* had been extracted from her vocabulary years ago and laid to rest in a rather elaborate ceremony.

"Those don't look like walking shoes to me, baby . . ."

"Oh, honey, I can walk in these shoes," she assured me.

"Are they comfortable?"

"Like walking on air," she promised.

"They don't look comfortable with that long skinny little spike," I said. "They look more like a weapon than a walking shoe. You probably couldn't even get past airport security wearing those suckers."

"Leave my spikes alone, honey. It'll be just fine. Come on."

Not even two hours into our afternoon, Molly was limping on one foot and practically crawling on the other.

"My feet are killing me," she grumbled.

"I told you about those shoes," I scolded, staring at her swollen ankles. This was typical Molly, the queen in her finest hour, always determined to do it *her* way even if it was the wrong way. She would rather die doing it the wrong way than to live doing it the right one.

"You should have told me we were going to the Poka Wahna Street Fair for Pete's sakes."

Poka Wanna County Street Fair was a celebration of mime, music, and art. There were poetry and dance competitions, step shows, theater presentations, mime performances, fanfare, and wild ridiculous celebration. I was in heaven because all of this creative energy was blowing my mind, but Molly on the other hand was nothing short of miserable.

"Damn. Damn," she mumbled consoling swollen toes. "Can we stop for a minute?" she snapped. As we paused for consolation, I scouted the area for an unoccupied bench, combing through the in-line skaters and baby strollers. We eased through congested crowds to make our way across the busy square filled with vendors and patrons. I pushed past circus clowns and sideshows, pulling Molly up from the rear of the crowd, hoping something would engage her enough to take the sour from her face.

"My feet, my feet," she continued to chant on my heels *and* on my nerves. We continued to make our way across the grassy area until I found an empty bench, where we stopped for refuge. As Molly sulked over her bruised feet, I noticed a mime in my peripheral vision. The mime was checking me out and how odd I thought he was. In the middle of whatever it is that mimes do, he stopped to stare at me. And of course this drew the attention of the large crowd that had gathered to watch his performance.

Don't look at me, I said to him in silence. *Don't look.* You'll only draw the eyes of strangers and I am not prepared to combat the molestation of foreign stares.

"Are you ready?" I asked Molly, slightly irritated.

"Not yet," she said fanning herself, making a big deal over plump breasts that she had squeezed into a T-shirt small enough to fit a toddler.

"That guy is staring at me," I said leaning into Molly.

"Honey, lots of guys stare at you," she said, looking the opposite direction, paying little attention to my discomfort.

"He's *not* just a guy, Molly. Look over there, the mime," I said trying to talk without moving my lips. "The whole crowd is staring at me now."

"They think you're cute," said Molly distracted. She was fixing her makeup, putting her boobs back in place, correcting her posture, dusting the powder off her nose, checking her lip liner, all the while I tried to disappear, but that would be one wish to go ungranted.

Before I could gather my composure the mime and his audience were standing before the bench Molly and I were sitting on. The mime motioned Molly to get up and she did. In turn, he took her seat and moved painfully close to me.

I moved away.

He scooted in.

And I moved farther away. And this little dance went on till one of my butt cheeks was hanging off the bench and the other was barely holding on. The crowd was getting big kicks off his routine and I was getting a headache. Why was he persecuting me like this?

"Leave me alone," I whispered to him in a soft voice. He didn't reply, but mimes never do. He just kept staring, taking it upon himself to peer around me, behind me, through me, and inside me.

"Leave me alone," I said again a little louder and this time I offered him a ten-dollar bill.

He panned the air like he was climbing a wall, making symbolic reference to the wall between us. And he stood up on the bench and climbed and climbed, like he was really going some-where. When he finished being dramatic he stopped, stood still, and knocked on the pretend door that didn't stand between us. The crowd was terribly amused by this and it looked ever so clever that even I broke with a partial smile. He proceeded to give me pretend flowers and motioned for me to smell them by smelling them first. And I obliged. Molly must have thought this was terribly cute because she had a grin on her face the size of all Montana.

"Okay," I said. "You win, you win."

He closed the pretend door and then offered a not-so-pretend kiss on the cheek. His lips were soft, gentle, honest. "Thank you," he whispered in my ear.

I felt something magical. This was not my typical response to men. There was something that drew me to him even though I did not wish to be drawn. I didn't want him to touch me but I did want to feel him. It was a paradoxical moment cemented in the anxiety of him making a theatrical mockery of my embar-rassment. When he left I was breathless, almost disoriented.

CHEMISTRY.

12

LIKE WATER

"Close your mouth," I directed Molly as her bottom lip almost hit the concrete. "You are so dramatic!" I added in summation to her response of the news that I had slept with Sky.

"You slept with him?" she squealed, drawing stares from onlookers inside the restaurant where we sat.

"You had sex with him, honey?" asked Molly dramatically. "I can't believe you did it. You really did it. I can't believe you did it. I'm dying over here," she continued. She went on so far as to tell a complete stranger passing by, "She slept with him . . . I can't believe it!"

I quickly covered her mouth with my hand.

"Would you *please* shut up!" I scolded. "You're embarrassing me!"

"I just can't believe it, baby," she continued as if she hadn't beaten it down enough already. "And I can't believe you waited so long to tell me. Why didn't you tell me before now?"

"Because I'm trying to forget about it," I replied, almost sulking.

"Uh-oh . . ." she said, frowning. "Sounds like you didn't really get into it."

"More the other way around," I said.

"He didn't get into it?".

"I don't think so," I said, defeated.

"What are you saying? It wasn't good? Don't leave me hanging like this," she whined.

"It was like making love to a woman," I said in a low voice.

"Really?" asked Molly looking stupid. "A woman? Was is that bad?"

"Worse," I confirmed.

"Damn."

"It felt really weird. I don't think he had ever been with a woman before."

"Oh, honey, don't you think you're exaggerating? How could he have not ever been with a woman before?"

"I don't know, maybe he was too busy being with a man," I said with a raised brow. "Food for thought," I added. "My psychic, Mabel, told me to be careful."

"Oh, come on, you're going to believe that crazy coot?"

"Call her what you want, but everything she says comes to pass."

"Hocus-pocus, shit," said Molly, irritated. "I can't believe you actually buy into that garbage."

"Gotta believe in something," I said in self-defense. "Right, Molly? What do you believe in?"

"I believe in lots of things," she snapped.

"Like what?" I challenged.

"Safe sex," she declared. "And shit that's based in reality," she continued. "Not that 'I'll charge you a chicken wing to read your fortune' bullshit."

Friction rose between us.

"Just admit it, you're a sucker for a one-legged con artist," she said in jest. "Do you know what Mabel is? A bad habit."

"Well, I guess you're the leading authority on bad habits seeing as you how you just got of rehab, *again*," I said, cutting her off at the knees. If there was going to be a stone-throwing contest, Molly was about to get a beat down. The situation could have worsened, but it didn't because the tiff ended there. It had to because if it didn't, the relationship would have expired, not today, but years ago. So in order to keep peace on earth and goodwill to all men, we often both jumped ship and called it even. I sucked up my blame and she soaked up hers. And it was always followed by a long beat of silence so that each party had sufficient time to discard bruised feelings and bulky egos.

Silence.

And a long beat.

"So," said Molly reentering the conversation, "you really think he's gay?"

"I don't know for sure," I said quietly.

"So what are you going to do?"

"I'll let you know when I figure it out."

"Have you seen him since that night?" she asked.

"In passing."

"So the relationship changed?" she asked.

"Of course the relationship changed," I said regretfully. "I slept with him."

I paused a moment to reflect on what a poor decision sleeping with him was and by the time I returned to reality, Molly had slipped into the women's restroom and altered her demeanor. When she reentered the restaurant she was staggering, mumbling. This was tradition with Molly Wood. She always celebrated her sobriety by getting smashed.

"Oh, shit," I said jumping to assist her. Molly was laughing and slurring. "Hoooneey . . . hooonney . . . feel like dancing? Feel like dancing?" she asked loud and disoriented.

I quickly ushered her to a seat.

"I wanna dance with somebody . . ." she sang, massacring Whitney's song. "With somebody who loves me." I tried to contain her animated performance because people were staring.

"Molly," I said. "Molly. Stop it," I said firmer.

"I've done all right up till now, but it's the light of the day that shows me how," she belted swinging her hips, caressing her breasts. Molly was in her own world. And she was dragging me there, too, against my will. Dirty old men were penetrating her with invasive eye contact. I tried to force her to sit down but she pushed me backward so hard that I almost lost my balance and fell. The only thing that saved me from the ground was the sharp edge of a table.

I couldn't get a grip on Molly. She couldn't even get a grip on herself. I faded into the silence of a loud background. I moved away from the pulse of the room while Molly flirted with a respectable-looking white guy who didn't seem so respectable at all once the two of them exited to the nearest restroom. And I didn't try to stop her. I rarely did. That's who she was, so I just let her be.

She had consumed so much alcohol that by morning I would be called upon to "fill in the blanks" of bad behavior. I would be asked to recite her evening course like the alphabet and I would oblige. I would be asked to relive the embarrassing moments and then be further asked to dismiss their magnitude. I grabbed for a seat at the bar. The contemplation of such ill-witted drama was drawing a migraine in the center of my forehead.

"You are the most beautiful woman in this room," said the stranger beside me. I sized him up as a closet pervert shielded by poor lighting.

"Thanks," I said, more sarcastic than appreciative.

"Each man decides his own fate," he said paying no attention to my mood.

"What?"

"Your friend over there," he said pointing to Molly. "She's on her own journey. It's not up to us to judge anybody else's journey."

"Okay, Aristotle," I shot back.

"It's true."

"You think I'm judging her?" I asked.

"Yes," he didn't hesitate to say.

"Well it doesn't matter what you think . . ."

"You're right," he said taking a sip of whatever he was drinking.

"I'm not judging her . . ." I couldn't leave it alone. "And why am I explaining myself to you?"

"Because you like me," he declared with disillusioned confidence.

"Yeah right . . ." I said, rolling my eyes.

"We've shared a moment, you and I."

"In your dreams . . ."

"Right out there," he said pointing to an empty bench in the grassy area.

"Oh," I said finally getting it. "You're the mime?"

He made the "my lips are sealed" motion with his fingers and I smiled as he slid from the dark corner into the light.

TIME
OUT

You know that moment in time that occurs when you see someone and they see you and you know that you should have seen them long before now because they are the most complete image of perfection you have ever seen? Well, this felt like one of those moments.

I'm not typically attracted to white men, but when I saw this man I wanted him. He was someone I wanted to possess or maybe someone I wanted to possess me, especially when he moved into the light and I saw how beautiful he was. It was then that insecurity emerged and did a jig on the table. I was suddenly self-conscious about everything from bad breath to dandruff. Was there pepper between my teeth from dinner? Was my hair in place? My posture correct? And deodorant still working?

My hands were up on the counter, down by my side, and up again because I just didn't know what to do with them. They were in the way, and if I didn't actually need them to drive myself home, I'd just as soon cut them off. But then, how would I logically explain an upper torso with two empty sockets where limbs *used* to be?

I got dizzy staring at him. His brown locks were tapered on the side. His arms were so well defined they screamed, "Yes, I have a current gym pass." His beautiful brown eyes were set deep inside his head. His eyebrows were thick and rich, arching on each end, almost meeting in the middle. His lips were big and juicy. White men "might" be able to jump, but they damn sure don't come with big, juicy lips. Do they? Though I *loved* his lips, it was his high-profile dimples that sealed the attraction. He had dimples deeper than the Grand Canyon.

Can I crawl on top of you right now?

His lips were moving because, after all, he was talking to me, but I was too busy consulting my imagination on the possibility of courting him to answer.

"What?" I asked, coming back to reality.

"What's your name?" he asked again.

"Michael," I said, extending my hand.

"Eddie," he said accepting it.

I was aware of the stupid grin on my face, but whatever the reason, I couldn't wipe it off. And it stayed there till 2 A.M.

And at 2:01 A.M., things took a turn for the worse.

I held Molly's hair as she threw up on the sidewalk. I had seen Molly smashed out of her gourd before, but I had never seen her this sick. Her shoes were dangling in my hands and the streets were as bare as her feet.

We were standing on the sidewalk in the dark trying to make our way back to the car. My moment with Eddie had come and gone because he had left more than an hour ago. As a matter of fact, the bulk of the normal people had already gone home, and all that was left behind were empty beer cans and rejects from the Betty Ford Clinic.

"Oh, Molly Wood," I said watching the eruption of fluids. "What's going on, Molly Wood?"

"Rehab . . . it's killing me. I used to be able to hold my liquor. Now look at me. I'm a lightweight," she moaned. "I am my mother's daughter," she belched raising an empty can of malt liquor upward. There was something about a bleached blonde white girl and a can of Colt 45 that didn't quite mix.

"To sobriety," I whispered under my breath. We ended up where we didn't want to be, or should I say where I didn't want to be, celebrating thirty days of Molly's sobriety by getting smashed.

Way to go, Molly.

"Do you love me, honey?" asked Molly. She always wanted to know if I loved her, as if my love really mattered.

"Do you love me?" she asked again like a child, searching

desperately for acceptance. "Love me," she mumbled under her breath. She rested a heavy head and heavier heart against my shoulder, appearing too weak to make the hike back to the car. I felt sorry for Molly, and, had she not weighed twenty-five pounds more than I, carrying her would have been option. But since I wasn't trying to throw my back out and scuff my new leather heels, Molly Wood would have to make it on her own.

She had taught me so much about life, love, and living. She was the greatest illusion I had ever known because she made living an empty life look full.

"I'll love you till the day I die or till the day I lose the meaning of love . . . whichever comes first," I reassured her.

And she cried.

And so did I.

We walked hand in hand like the soul mates that we were.

"I'm ready to blow this Popsicle stand . . . where's the goddamned car, honey?" she asked, then burped.

"It seems like it's on the other side of the world."

And it took us about thirty-seven minutes in the dark and cold to walk to the other side of the world.

13

CAVEMAN STYLE

He should have never taken "it" out, and I should have never taken "it" on.

Antonio.

South American boy toy.

He was old enough to know better, young enough to do it all.

Twenty-one years old.

Hot.

Sculpted.

Naive.

Insatiable.

Sensuous.

Erotic.

He met the criteria again and again. He had no natural aptitude toward intelligence, but then I was too fond of his sex to call him *stupid* lest he cut me off.

He was my distributor, an equalizing force willing to match endurance against his supply, my demand. Our conversation was minimal. As a matter of fact, I don't even think he spoke English. But then again, syntax was not my primary interest in his being.

Antonio worked when I tired of my vibrator. And when I needed to feel skin, warmth, flesh, and more—I called him to me.

No questions.

No answers.

Just condoms, if you will. Yes, condoms, because I wasn't on the pill. The pill made me bloated and crazy.

We didn't have anything. We just had a *thing*. And as long as I had a vested interest in the equipment he possessed and the way he had learned to use it, he would always be around. And so would I.

At twenty-one, Antonio was in heat all year-round. Seduction was his second occupation, but his primary source of income was busing tables. And that's where I met him two years ago at the deep end of a Cuban hole in the wall.

"Mama mia," I uttered as he refilled my water. "Put me out and pour me out," I whispered under my breath. And though he couldn't have heard me or understood the English of my words, somehow he knew what I wanted.

I communicated my animal urges caveman style, gyrating my vibrations without making a move. And just like a movie, that night we swapped interchangeable moans while I taught him my language and he taught me his. And though we rarely spoke to one another, a lot was always said. And every time we meet and greet caveman style, I vow that I'll never do it again. At some point *celibacy* should have been my second occupation, but I never went long enough without sex to achieve it.

I always intend for the ride to end and temporarily it does. Antonio comes and *comes*, then goes. He goes on with his life and I go on with mine. But when the flames get too hot for extinction on my own, I am forced to call him back, feed him pizza, and swallow him whole.

In theory, we swap empty, meaningless sex for a moment of pleasure. It is a moment that never lasts beyond the last rub and the weakest throb of my strongest orgasm, but theory never cramped my style.

One time he asked in his own way, did it bother me that he didn't care for me? A question too deep for two people, who temporarily disconnect from their minds and hearts to answer.

Does it bother me that he doesn't care for me? No. But it bothers me that *no ones* cares for me. Antonio is a nameless face on a beautiful body automatically programmed to dial my channel and tune my vibe. And only after his visit does the clarity he brings show so much distortion in my world.

Antonio offers me nothing except that he is willing to do for me what I cannot do for myself, satisfying sexual urges too large for my consumption. Beyond that I want nothing more from him and am willing to offer the same.

When he leaves, I return to my body, soul, and mind, and the emptiness eats me alive without the courtesy of anesthesia. Mastering the moments, I have not yet learned to balance all that is in between them. And that is why I have often found myself being led by the tongue like a dog in heat.

I vow after each meaningless exchange to reclaim my womanhood and honor my body by dismissing myself from the school of "bump and grind." I trade my hoochie outfit for a scholarly one, all the while mapping maneuvers to make my sexuality less scandalous.

I have struggled my entire life to contain my sexuality and I am usually able to sustain myself until I feel a throbbing sensation between my legs that won't dissipate. And it is then that I am forced to contemplate scandal. It is only when I feel that I will surely explode without a touch, moan, cry, and gush that I break down and call Him and Him and Him to me. And the damn shame of it is, they come. They come, stay a beat, strip away all that makes me whole, and depart with the pieces leaving me stuck with a belly full of sperm and a bad attitude.

14

STILL BEATING

One night after Antonio left, I had not even dried up yet before the phone rang. I answered the line trying to sound more like a virgin than a woman who had just had her brains screwed out.

"Hello?"

"Michael?" an unfamiliar voice asked.

"This is she."

"Michael, it's Eddie."

I was so overwhelmed by the sound of his voice that I bit my tongue and started jumping up and down in the same place.

It's him.

It's him.

It's him.

Naked and jiggling, I spun around the room like an exhibitionist.

"Eddie!" I screamed, giving insight into desperation, but desperation is unattractive, so I tried to clean it up by sounding less enthusiastic. "Oh, yes, Eddie . . ."

"How have you been?" he asked.

"Good," I said first and reaffirmed a second time trying desperately to convince myself. "Really good."

It's too early in the game to let him know I'm mentally unstable. It would look pathetic on the first phone call to pour out my problems like ketchup, allowing them to bleed through the conversation. *My mood has more downs than ups. I live paycheck to paycheck because I am a Shop-O-Holic. The last time I tried to cook a nutritious meal the building had to be evacuated because my apartment caught on fire. I am religiously conflicted and can't decide if I want to follow Buddha or Jesus. If a man has two legs and a penis there's a high probability that I've slept with him. No, scratch that last sentence because legs aren't necessary, if a man has a penis there's a high probability I've slept with him. Are you sure you want to get to know me?*

"You've been on my mind lately," he said. "I'm very attracted to you."

Lost for words, I could only respond, "Thanks."

"Are you attracted to me?"

"Wow, you're direct."

"I'm honest," he said.

"And I'm shy," I tossed out for closure.

"You don't seem very shy at all."

"You don't know me well enough to make assumptions—"

"But I'd like to," he cut me off before I could even get started.

"Gee, you don't waste any time."

"This isn't a marriage proposal, it's just an invitation."

"To what?" I had to ask.

"To get to know me."

I wanted to pretend that I was holding out for a better offer, but before I could disengage mouth from brain I blurted, "Yes."

"Yes?" he asked for clarification.

"Yes," I said a little softer the second time so I wouldn't sound so desperate, at least not right away. We all want to be independent of our instincts and represent that we're taller than our actual reflection.

"You'll go out with me?" he asked.

"Yes, I'll go out with you."

I did all of the things I typically do before a big date, namely call Molly for moral support.

"It's going down," I told her.

"First date?"

"First date."

"All right," she said. "Let's roll through the checklist."

"Okay," I replied.

"Facial?"

"Check."

"Manicure and pedicure?"

"Of course."

"What about the hair?"

"Exquisite," I not so humbly replied.

"Shave the legs?"

"Check."

"Above the knee?"

"For this guy, yes," I said.

"Did you wax the lips?"

"I don't have a mustache . . ."

"I wasn't talking about *those* lips," she said.

"Oh," I quickly replied embarrassed. "I trimmed."

"Well, sounds like you're ready," she said.

"Really?" I asked, my confidence beginning to falter.

"Michael," she said annoyed, "this guy could be your prince . . . what are you so afraid of?"

"Nothing," I said, trying to blow off what could easily turn into a serious conversation. And I wasn't in the mood for serious.

"Bullshit," insisted Molly. "What are you so afraid of . . . a happy ending?"

I laughed.

I couldn't help it.

Molly Wood actually made sense sometimes. But it was a sad appraisal in my estimation because she made sense of my life when she was sober and sense of her own only when she was high. And that was such a waste of what once was a brilliant mind to begin with.

"I'll call you tomorrow," I told her. "I love you, girl."

"Ditto," she replied.

When I hung up the phone I scurried around my apartment putting the finishing touches on a look that I wasn't sure would fly. I had done everything to prep till there was nothing left to do except die waiting for one of the most beautiful men I've ever met to arrive at my doorstep and ring my bell. Well, perhaps there were other things to do, like stand in the mirror and stare at the finished product. A caramel-colored woman with gray to green eyes wearing a tight jean skirt with a cotton top that cropped in the front, tied in the back. Laced sandals, straw tote bag, and a matching hat.

But was it enough?

Facing my reflection in the mirror, I reached out to touch the glass and beg the streak-free structure for kindness.

Am I enough?

Am I truly enough?

I tilted my head to the left, right, up, then down. I studied my profile from every angle I could get my neck to twist. My eyes, nose, lips, brow, butt, waist, legs, thighs, curves, and heart.

Am I *enough?*

The irony turned me like a rusted knob and I exhaled. It was a long, deep, and drawn breath. There was nothing but truth staring me in the face. And the truth was as long as there were at least two women breathing, one would always be prettier. I could spend my life savings primping and prepping, transform-ing myself into the personification of walking beauty, then step outside and *Wham!* There she goes, twice as beautiful with half the work. How's that slam back to reality?

There will always be someone more beautiful than me, it will be *you,* and someone more beautiful than you and it will be *her.* And even the most beautiful one of us all will be outdone by a younger and more supple version of herself.

I relied so heavily on my face and figure to pull in the crowd, the compliments, the attention, the men, and the boy toys, that I forgot every now and again to take inventory of my heart, just to make sure it was still beating.

"Are you still there?" I whispered to my heart, making no quick assumption that it was.

I couldn't stop my eyes from twitching and my feet from tapping the floor. I couldn't stop fidgeting, shifting positions, salivating. I could barely look at him, but I couldn't stand not to look because he was so majestic in his appearance.

I was insanely attracted.

Insanely.

He was beautiful without the arrogance, sensitive yet still heterosexual, going places, but still down to earth. And when he spoke to me he actually looked into my eyes and not at my breasts, a skill worthy of extra bonus points. He was a gentleman without being a nerd. An intelligent conversationalist without being a know-it-all. He held my door, my hand and all of my attention.

On our first date I learned his last name was Matsen. He was thirty-one and the eldest of four children. His mother was a waitress and his father, a magician. According to Eddie the best trick his father ever did was "going to the store for a gallon of milk and then disappearing." Eddie was seven years old and he never saw his father again. The rest of his siblings were like a stepladder: six, four, two, and one.

After Eddie's father disappeared, his mother became the

driving force in the family, and Eddie stepped up to take on the role as husband/daddy.

"I skipped childhood," he admitted in jest, but beneath his true confession there was pain. "I went from wearing diapers to smoking cigars and balancing checkbooks."

"How did you know how to balance a checkbook?" I asked.

"Same way I learned to smoke a cigar, trial and error."

I laughed.

"It was cool though," Eddie said. "My mother was a good lady. She kept the ship afloat, you know."

"Yeah," I said. "I do know actually."

"Where is your mother now?" I asked.

"Nursing home," he said.

"Do you visit much?" I asked.

"Not as much as I should," he replied. "She doesn't recognize me anymore. Alzheimer's."

"I'm sorry," I said reaching for his hand. "Where are your siblings?"

"Two in Denver. One in Portland."

"Are you close?"

He shrugged but didn't answer and that told me everything.

"Do you regret missing your childhood?" I asked him.

"No," he replied quicker than I thought he would. "Childhood was a burden."

Woah.

"Tell me about your childhood." he said.

I locked my heart and he must have heard the click.

"We don't have to talk about it," he said reassuringly.

"No, it's not that," I said lying, because it was *that*. What could I possibly say about my childhood?

My mother was koo-koo when I was young. Now she's a Jesus freak. My father accidentally killed himself, but I think he died on purpose. And by the way, I'm crazy, too. Nice meeting you. I'm sure you'll never call again. Or I could just settle for something simple like, "I had a childhood obsession with 'Goldilocks and the Three Bears.' My papa read me that book faithfully every night till . . ." I paused, then dropped off before detouring with, "I never learned how to ride a bike. My mother tried to teach me how to ride a bike once and that was a disaster."

"I'll teach you," he volunteered eagerly.

"What if I fall?"

"I'll catch you."

"What if I accidentally ride off a cliff?" I asked, posing a more challenging scenario.

"Then I'll teach you to fly."

"Whoa," was all that I could say.

In dating situations I tend to believe that most people will attempt to find out what you like and become it. But Eddie broke down who he was and left it up to me to accept it. He didn't give me multiple choice nor did he leave me to fill in the blank. In every line and under every breath, I felt as though he said, "This is me."

Being with him was like meeting normal for the first time. The guys I usually dated ranged from ex-cons to illegal aliens, so this was a magnificent departure from the usual suspects.

"Where are we going?" I asked as we sped down the highway.

"It's a surprise," he winked as he held my hand.

"A surprise?" I smiled.

"Do you like surprises?" he asked.

"Good ones," I said.

"What's your definition of a good surprise?" he asked.

A negative HIV test, but I couldn't very well say that now, could I?

"Hmmmm . . . a good surprise . . . when the IRS owes you instead of the other way around," I said proudly for thinking on my feet. He looked at me with such a blank stare that I leaned into him and whispered, "Were you searching for something a little more earth shattering?"

After that statement, there was nothing but laughter filling dead spaces where conversation had dropped off. Even his laugh was attractive and all I could do was grip the sides of the door and pray that I didn't dissolve, spilling onto the seats of his jeep and ruining the leather.

"Your turn," I said. "What's your definition of a good surprise?"

"My definition of a good surprise?" he asked, squeezing my hand tighter. "You," he said without batting an eye.

And just like that the mood changed.

"Me?" I stared into the steamy bathroom mirror, pinching myself to make sure I was still breathing after the date had ended.

Not only was he beautiful, compassionate, energetic, and insightful, he was also employed, owned his own ride, and came to the date prepared with real money and not Monopoly cash. When he spoke, he actually had something to say. He wasn't like the typical guys I dated, all graduates of the "Mack School of One-Liners."

He could look at me, through me, beyond me, and around me. He could find my vibe and feel my vibe. He could ride me like a wave without laying a hand on my body. He could mesmerize, fantasize, and harmonize against my skin. When I was with him I felt no compromise of my womanhood. He wanted to know me and was willing to go with me on whatever tangent I temporarily embraced. He cut through my defenses and left me breathless without saying a word.

He was white and I was black, not my usual combination, but nobody seemed to care. And as much as I liked Eddie, initially I was uncomfortable about the skin difference. Black women didn't typically entertain white men. At least none of the black women I knew. And as for the white guys I knew, they were usually chasing California blondes all over town, even though we were in Shilo, Colorado. I had wondered if my brown skin was too black for Eddie or if his fair skin would be too pale for me. But on our first date, the only color in question seemed to be red. We had gone cherry picking followed by a picnic at the top of a hill where Eddie broke out with the ultimate Mack move, lunch on a blanket. As he pulled wine, cheese, and appetizers from the basket, I stood in amazement asking myself the tough question: *Is this guy for real?*

"Can I help?" I asked, offering my assistance while he prepared our meal.

"No," he said.

"I feel like I need to do something," I said a little fidgety.

"Just be," he said gently.

"No one has ever—" I started, then stopped.

"Ever what?" he asked digging up nerves without knowing it.

"Never mind," I replied, switching gears. I wouldn't want him to think ill of me so early on by breaking down my truth. Papa was the only man who had ever suggested that "I just be" until Eddie came along. But I didn't want to frighten Eddie by saying, "Hey, you remind me of my dead father." And I certainly didn't want him to think that I was as "needy" as I would one day grow to be. For all intents and purposes, needy was a part of my nature.

"Thank you for today," I whispered.

And whispered.

And whispered.

Till I realized the date was over and Dorothy was back in Kansas. I was standing in the bathroom mouthing words with no sound and feeling for my heart to make sure it was still beating.

15

TREKKING TEARS

The last Sunday of every month for the past four years Sky and I had always done brunch. So how could we skip brunch this month? Could we suspend it on the basis that we accidentally slept together and destroyed our friendship? Could we postpone till our bodies returned to their preintercourse condition? Seated across from one another, we both looked guilty, denying the obvious.

"We blew it, didn't we?" I asked as we sat on the terrace of one of my favorite restaurants. And though I tried not to look and sound bitter, somehow I am not convinced that I was successful in the translation. The corners of my mouth curled unexpectedly and my jaw hung lower than I had hoped it would.

Sky appeared uncomfortable and ill-prepared to discuss the matter. I feared one more word on this touchy topic would send him searching for an emergency exit. Avoidance is the dance of the man who has not yet learned to discharge his best friend without hurting her feelings. *Too late, feelings already hurt.*

He picked at his plate, pouring good emotions over a chile

omelet. "This is the best omelet in town," he boasted, trying to ignore my vibe.

I nodded.

"How's work?" he asked.

"Dead," I answered sarcastically.

He laughed. It was nervous laughter, and nervous laughter gets my goat every time.

"How is your mother?"

"Fine," I said, becoming more irritated by the minute. *Why are you completely ignoring this?* I wanted to scream, but didn't have the guts.

I put my fork down, crossed my arms, and gave him the look.

He saw the look and glanced away.

"You're not going to talk to me, are you?" I confronted him dead on.

"We're talking," he shot back with attitude. "What's your problem?" He tried to look mean, pissed off, disjointed, and bent out of shape. But he was just plain old scared.

"I have the same problem you have," I said.

"I don't have any problems," he said.

"Well . . . you're either stupid or in denial," I said.

He didn't appreciate that.

"Sky," I pleaded. "I just want things to be the way they used to be."

"Well, you're either stupid or in denial . . . things will never be the same again," he said.

I leaned across the table and asked him point blank, "Why did you do it?"

"Do what?" he asked with a mouth full of egg.

"Sleep with me."

"You wanted me to," he accused, spraying bitterness between my eyes. *And it stung.*

"I wanted you to?" I asked with my back arched and the rest of me tilted forward, prepared for the attack.

"You wanted me to," he said, so slowly and articulately that it felt as if he were pouring alcohol on an open cut.

"Oh great . . . a mercy lay. Well, I guess you've done your good deed for this lifetime. I wonder how many brownie points you get with Jesus for a mercy lay."

"I knew you couldn't handle it. That's why I didn't want to talk about it," he said, throwing his fork down on the plate, drawing the attention of strangers who had probably already overheard bits and pieces of a maddening conversation.

Mercy lay.

You wanted me to.

Denial and stupid.

These were all key components in a conversation that had already begun tearing at my heart. Might as well rip open my chest and leave the beating organ on the table as part of the waiter's tip.

I was struggling to look unaffected, but my face was an open book to disappointment, hurt, anger, sadness, and regret. I was hoping to look bland; instead I felt ridiculous and hollow, suddenly conscious of my awkwardness.

"It never lasts," he said, sounding like the judge and the jury. "It never lasts longer than a night. Guy after guy after guy. You fall in love every other day hoping every loser that you allow between your legs will be the one. This one, that one, or the other one. You take ridiculous chances and make bets on long-shots that you know won't pay off. Your heart falls apart, then you put it back together, mending it best you can . . . only to have it fall apart again, too soon. Every time I look at your face I feel your pain," his voice softens to the point of an apology. "The night we slept together . . . I didn't want you to be alone. I didn't want you to get high on a temporary fix. I didn't want you to go home and make a call to some bastard who's just using you," his voice trailed off.

By the time he finished speaking, my nose was bright red and I was crying because I knew I was a fool.

I knew there was truth in Sky's testimony, but I had been too busy denying its existence. I rationalized that if I denied the truth long enough, perhaps Jesus would grant me enough time to make it right. Deep down inside, I sold myself cheap in an attempt to raise my value.

Damn.

It didn't work.

So no surprise when my chest cavity opened, unable to bear the weight of its bruises, and dumped out my heart involuntarily right beside the ham and eggs.

"You always pick the wrong guy," Sky said gently. "Including me."

I continued to cry, my head lowered. I didn't even have the strength to pull it back up, or eat, or move, breathe, sigh, gasp, or fall out onto the floor.

Sky got up from his seat, knelt beside me, and wrapped himself around me, holding me. People were staring, but he didn't care and neither did I.

I loved him and he knew it. He succumbed to my loneliness, but in doing so, dishonored his own flesh and resented me in the process. He gave himself to me so I wouldn't have to give myself to someone else. He gave me love out of pity and took it back out of resentment. He manipulated Mother Nature, changed the course of our friendship, and in the end, we all ended up losing.

When we exited the restaurant arm in arm, I knew our friendship was different and that it would never be the same again. But I also knew more strongly than ever it definitely wasn't over yet.

16

THE SHADOW OF MY STUPID

In the meantime, Eddie kept calling and I kept returning his calls.

He continued to share himself with me and I continued to give myself away.

He came.

Went.

And came again.

And in between visits I felt "needy" emerge and I was left victimized by its withdrawals. And that's what I'm going through now. Every time Eddie leaves me, I crave him till we meet again. Upon parting, I experience temporary anxiety where I am not quite able to catch my breath. It's an edgy feeling of nervous energy distributed a little too far to the left, a little too far to the right. It's nights lacquered in insomnia. I hold out my hand and watch it tremble because I just can't be still. I can't decide on a mood, so I remain perpetually stuck between irritability and euphoria. It's like waiting on something great and catastrophic to happen at the same moment, in the same breath. It's like feeling full even when I haven't eaten because the growing pit in my stomach demands space in place of food. At the core of my withdrawals, I peek through illusion to discover crave lurking at the base of my disturbance. *Oh God and I have to hide it because he hates a needy woman.*

I'm starting to get addicted to him. I hate being an addict, but then again, being an addict really turns me on. I get a rush from dancing on the edge and a bigger rush from falling off. It's not the crash that I enjoy, but the sensation of falling that makes me feel alive. Sick, isn't it?

Eddie has been a constant energy in my life for seven weeks. I have settled into the groove of him being there. He calls daily and not only do I anticipate his calls, I wait for them, ache for them. I look forward to them and depend upon them to provide me with a heavy dose of intoxication to float me through my day. Pathetic, I know.

Did I mention it has been seven weeks? I have gone a full seven weeks without sex? Eddie and I have not swapped body fluids yet. His juices remain in his domain and mine are resting comfortably in my own. Actually "resting" would be an inappropriate term to describe the volcanic buildup between my legs. On any given moment I am prepared to explode without warning. When I step, I step lightly lest I come and spontaneously combust all in the same breath.

I have abandoned the sacred practice of masturbation. I want a fresh start and an honest orgasm for a change.

Eddie is an upstanding companion. He visits three to four

times a week bringing food, laughter, and stimulation. He's so decent it scares me. When he leaves, he gives me a gentle kiss on the forehead, never going for the lips.

What the? . . .

Okay. So I am ultraconservative with him, too. He knows I'm not the Virgin Mary, but I don't want him to think my middle name is "Lucy Goosey" either. I even tossed out my sex toys. No let me rephrase that—*tossed out* sounds so final. I simply hid them from plain view. I wasn't trying to change my life, just trying to change the way I lived.

Most of the men I've dated in the past were detours *away* from happiness. My longest relationship to date lasted eight months and when it was all said it done the sum of that relationship equaled nothing more than a one-night stand. The only difference was it took us eight months to reach the end of the long, dark night.

The moment I met Eddie, I felt like hope hopped on the back of a wooden horse and trotted to my footsteps. And even though his love showed up with anxiety flaming under its belly, I was grateful for its arrival. Desperation is such a naughty word in the single woman's vocabulary, but naughty was how I felt and desperate wasn't the half of it. Eddie felt like my *last* chance to have something real. No one had stayed as long as he had nor reciprocated with such intensity. No one since Papa had ever loved me so completely, and I couldn't lose that again. Deep down inside I felt that no one would ever care again, and if they did care again they wouldn't care like *this*. I also knew that if I worked it right, there would be no reason that I should have to die alone.

One night while Eddie and I lay in each other's arms he did something *amazing*.

"Come with me," he whispered pulling me off the couch and toward the front door.

"Baby, I'm tired," I tried to complain, but he wasn't listening. When we got to the front door he had another request.

Close your eyes.

What?

Close them.

Okay. He was cute enough "play along," so I closed them.

He opened the front door and pulled me to its edge.

"Don't run me into a wall, Eddie."

"Open," he commanded.

When I opened my eyes I couldn't believe it! A beautiful bike was sitting at my doorstep with a big red bow sitting on top of the handlebars.

"What?" I exclaimed circling the apparatus. "What is this?"

Eddie leaned against the door with a painted smile on his face looking rather pleased with himself.

"You bought me a bike?" I asked, astounded by his generosity. "Oh my God . . ."

I didn't even know what to say.

No one had ever been that kind or gracious.

No one had ever been that considerate or *human*.

"I love you . . ." I spilled, then froze because I wanted to take it back. It was too soon for such a heavy proclamation, such a powerful declaration. But I loved him, and more important, I felt loved *by* him and maybe that's why I said it. All of these years I had been looking for someone to love me the way my papa did before he and Jack Daniel's became such good friends. In all honesty, I had been searching for a replacement, but there were no takers up until now. Or at least I thought so.

"I'm sorry," I said under my breath looking away.

"For what?" he asked sincerely, and of course I didn't respond, just changed the subject because it was easier.

"So you gonna give me a ride or what?" I asked, referring to the bicycle.

"Tomorrow," he said, pulling me back into the house, wooing me with his "know-how."

As we fell back onto the couch and into each other's arms, I began to reflect on all the things that created my beliefs. I have always envisioned my family portrait to include a chocolate man, but as it stands today, my would-be husband reflects coloring similar to that of the stale marshmallows in my cabinet. Perhaps I'm getting ahead of myself just a bit. Reality dictates that we have courted less than two months, and I should probably wait until he actually kisses me on the lips before I start naming our children.

"What are you thinking about?" he asked, stroking the ends of my hair, which lay draped across his chest like black satin.

You, me, and a June wedding, but of course I didn't say that.

"Nothing," I lied.

He didn't say anything in reply, just stared at me till his pupils glazed.

"Are we having a Kodak moment?" I asked, trying to break the serious groove that was stirring up around us. I hadn't realized it up to that moment, but I was scared, really scared. I liked this guy and didn't want to blow it by being too needy. I didn't want to give too much away or hold back more than I should.

"It's definitely a moment," he replied as he escorted his lips in the direction of my face. I froze and my respiring flesh turned stonelike. Last-minute jitters generated heat that flushed my cheeks to crimson. I hovered around two conditions: hysteria and a coma.

"What happens next?" I whispered.

My sexuality fell apart at the seams and I felt virginlike again. I circled confusion trying to remember what should sit up and what should be lying down. I was too disoriented to acknowledge what should be wet and what would be better suited remaining dry.

I had questions, but no answers, and he had answers, but no questions. So we met in the middle when he offered a slow grind that began on the base of my neck and worked its way up to the side of my cheek. His soft, black-man lips were pulsating as he gently followed my jawline to find the most sensitive of soft tissue, the lips.

He hit the spot, and the spot hit back.

"Mmmmmmmmmm," I moaned.

He withdrew a beat and then came back for more.

He offered his tongue.

I accepted.

I could feel him shifting positions as he gently mounted on

top and I slid underneath him. He climbed me like Mount Everest, strategically balancing his body weight against my chest.

Erotica had gone mad.

My heart was beating a thousand times per minute or perhaps it had stopped moving and wasn't beating at all. My stomach disengaged and my intestines took a turn for the worse, convulsing and twisting themselves into pretzellike shapes.

Are we going to? . . .

Or not? . . .

The kissing, rubbing, touching, and grinding had become so intense that I didn't know how to compose, maintain, or abstain anymore.

"Oh, God," I spilled with sound lacking in breath. I unsnapped my bra and slid it down past my breasts. And just like that he stopped. In the height of his arousal, he stopped. With the cessation of movement, I felt sudden disapproval. I buried my head into his chest because I was too afraid to look up and seek an explanation.

His body shifted and the weight fell off when he quietly slid off me and onto the couch. I kept my eyes shut and rolled into a ball. I didn't want to know why he stopped short of going all the way. I didn't want to trip on my insecurities, which by the way, were multiplying like cockroaches.

He wanted to stroke my face, but I pushed his hand away as I tried to hold the tears on the inside of my eyes, but I failed and the water began to fall.

"Why are you crying?" he asked.

"Vulnerability is a bitch," I said, without much emotion.

I got off the couch, deposited my breasts back into their respective holding places, and walked into the kitchen and began cleaning up.

He didn't say much after that.

We were at the crossroads of our relationship, and it had taken us seven weeks to get there. I feared that I was traveling by way of a jumbo jet and he was on a skateboard. Did I arrive at the gate *that* much quicker than he did?

My mode of transportation was fueled by desperation and a wilting womb. His snaillike motion was fueled by commitment anxiety and a reproduction ability that could sustain itself well into his seventies.

Where are you? I wanted to know, but felt too gutless to ask.

Why don't relationships ever cross the finish line at the same time? I could go on and on, as a matter of fact I did, till Eddie interrupted me. "So tomorrow night, right?" he asked.

"Tomorrow?" I asked, spinning myself out of the refrigerator where I had just spent the last nine minutes searching for comfort food. "Tomorrow?" I asked again.

"Your mother's . . ."

"Oh . . ." I said. "Oh . . . dinner," I repeated, fanning myself dramatically.

"You okay?" he asked.

"Yes," I lied at first, then took it back for truth. "No, Eddie . . . I'm not."

"What's wrong?"

"What are we doing?" I asked searching for the answer to that question all women want to know after the first date.

"What do you mean?" he asked with the same level of igno-rance that all men manage to hold on to. The use of the word *we* too early on *could* be a deal breaker.

"Do you like me, Eddie?" a voice from inside my body asked that felt disconnected from the rest of me. Asking someone if he "likes you" is like sitting your heart in the middle of the dance floor. Was I ready to be stomped to death? *Again?*

"I'm nuts about you, Michael. What? You're feeling insecure because I haven't jumped your bones yet?"

I didn't want to nod and look cheesy so I just rolled my eyes.

"I need to spend a little time getting used to the water before I ride the waves," he said. "The minute a man takes it upon himself to make love to a woman the tides change. I just want to make sure that when they change, they shift in the right direction."

He offered a gentle kiss on the forehead—always the fore-head, always the forehead. "See you tomorrow," he whispered leaving me standing in the kitchen propped against the shadow of my stupid.

17

THE *C*-WORD

Okay.

So here's the story.

Eddie is accompanying me to my mother's house today for dinner. As a matter of fact, we're on our way. As I speak, I am riding quietly on the passenger's side of his Jeep Cherokee. And there are two reasons that he and I are not dialoguing at this very moment: 1) I am having a conversation with myself, and 2) I'm still turned off about last night.

So, in just a few minutes I will be done speaking to myself, and at that point I will be available to reenter real-life conversation if I chose to do so. Now, whether or not I will actually choose to speak to *him* remains a mystery. At this particular moment my nerves are unraveled. And this, too, could be for several reasons:

1) If not properly sedated, my mother could be mistaken for strange.

2) I didn't quite know how to break the news that Eddie wasn't

black, which means I accidentally forgot to tell her that he was white. Oops.

3) I didn't tell Eddie that my mother was black, but I am taking a leap of faith that naturally he assumes that already.

"You're so quiet today," he suggested, squeezing my hand.

"I'm okay," I said, trying to look as pitiful on the outside as I felt on the inside.

"So tell me something about your mother," he said.

"Her last name is the same as mine," I said sarcastically. *Are you feeling my groove, bruised feelings, and poor attitude?* "What else is there?" I asked, pulling my hand back for safekeeping.

"Did you tell her who I was?" he asked.

"How can I tell her something I don't know?" I asked, pouting a bit.

"What do you mean by that?" he asked defensively.

"Who am I supposed to tell people you are? My friend? My boyfriend? My lover?"

"Okay, so you want a label now? Is that what this is about?" he asked. "Why do women do that? Can't they just let things evolve naturally?"

"Not when their eggs are being shot down by B-52 bombers. Women don't have the luxury of time. They can't push babies out of their birth canals at the age of ninety," I replied sarcastically.

"You have a great sense of humor," he said, trying to lighten the mood. And I went along with it because this was a given— *you get more flies with honey.*

"I'm witty," I said. "And charming. And ready . . ."

"For what?" he asked.

"To give you everything you want," I replied without hesitation.

His brow raised.

"And need," I concluded.

"I don't even know what I need," he said.

"Then let's figure it out together," I offered. "We're such a good team, you and I."

Eddie looked so nervous that his brow began to perspire.

"It's okay, baby," I said rubbing his shoulder with my hand, trying to calm his anxious nerves.

"Do you want the fairy tale, Michael? Because I'm not sure if I can give you that," he said sheepishly.

"No," I said softly. "The real-life Cinderella withered waiting for someone to love her. Juliet was bipolar. Romeo was a sociopath. And the only reason Alice was in Wonderland in the first place was because she was high on Prozac. Long story short, there's no such thing as a fairy tale."

"So what do you want?" he asked me point blank.

"More," it didn't take me but a moment to respond.

"Meaning?" he asked.

"*You*," I concluded.

"I'm not the fairy tale," he said.

"And I'm not the princess," I responded.

"Then what does that make us?" he asked, desperately seeking an answer.

"*Human*."

Silence.

Silence.

Silence.

Then he slowly nodded, defeated, "Okay. Okay," he said.

I kissed him gently on the lips.

If victories were to be decided by judge and jury, it was clear that I had won that day. In retrospect, it seemed like an unfair win. I had blindsided him into a commitment, begging him out of a piece of his heart that should have never been given away. But he did give it away and I would hold him to it from that day forward.

I got my dream.

Got my wish.

I managed to play Cinderella by changing her name.

I got my man.

Got my sustenance.

Got my way.

I got my right. I had assumed I won the *C*-word. A commitment. But little did I know the future has a way of snatching our victories away and replacing them with defeat.

18

GUESS WHO'S COMING TO DINNER?

We had been there just under an hour and the conversation was held to a minimum, except, of course, the excessive chatter from the meddling people from my mother's congregation: Sister Bula, her unattractive son, Boom Boom, and the church gossip queen, Drunetta. Funny thing about Drunetta, she was the quiet, shy type, but don't let the smooth taste fool you. Drunetta may have depicted the image of a deaf-mute, but she was the biggest blabbermouth in town.

Eddie and I sat on one end and everybody else sat on the other. In fact, so oddly were we placed that I began to feel as though we were on display.

Look at the happy little interracial lovebirds, I could almost hear them mocking. A feast had been prepared, but the mood was anything but festive and no matter how hard I tried to knock down the walls, new ones were being erected quicker than I could discard of the old.

"So," Bula said to Eddie, already instigating. "How do you make your living?"

"I'm a counselor," Eddie said smiling, trying to be polite to big fat Bula.

"Um–hmmmm," said Bula suspiciously. "Who you been counseling?"

"Teens in crisis."

"Ummmm," she responded. "How long you been doing that?"

"About a year," he replied.

"What did you do the year before that?" she asked.

"I was a performance artist for a local theater group," he said.

"How long you do that?" she asked again.

"A year."

"So . . . what did you do the year before that?" asked big-nosed Boom Boom, who by the way had a crush on me that dated all the way from seventh grade.

"I worked at a photography studio."

"How long you do that?" asked Bula. But before he could even reply she inserted, "Let me guess . . . about a year."

"No," said Eddie gently, "that gig lasted about six months."

Mother moaned.

Drunetta shot a look to Mother and Bula rolled her eyes.

Eddie was swift in catching their disapproval. "What? You don't like photography?" he asked playfully.

"We don't like instability," said my mother, her tone dripping with disapproval. "Seems like you got yourself a different job every year."

"Mother," I said to interrupt the flow. I felt as if they were about to pummel Eddie.

"Oh, Lord," said Bula, fanning her big ass. "Let's lighten up the mood 'round here. Boom Boom pass the collard greens."

He passed the greens and I prayed to Jesus that my family and their friends would not embarrass me in front of Eddie. By now I was trying to figure out why I had brought Eddie here in the first place. Was it because I wanted to show them that I was at least trying to do my part to close the gap between being single and being single *forever*?

"So Freddie . . ." said Boom Boom.

"It's Eddie," I corrected him with attitude.

Boom Boom pouted. "How long you been dating Michael?"

"A couple months," replied Eddie.

Mother grabbed at her chest and moaned. Dramatics were never too far away.

"Are you all right, Mother?" asked Drunetta.

"I'm okay," she said faintly.

Of course, I rolled my eyes.

"So you like black girls?" Boom Boom asked with a hard look in his eyes.

"Knock it off!" I snapped.

All eyes landed on me, then did a slow crawl to Eddie. Heads lowered and dinner resumed slowly. I mouthed the word "sorry" to Eddie. He reached for my hand, holding it a beat, which only made the natives more uncomfortable than they already were.

"You know, Eddie," Boom Boom said cautiously, "this is the white man's world. He can get anything he wants. As a matter of fact, he pretty much takes what he wants."

"What is your problem?" I asked throwing my fork down on my plate.

"I don't like to see the white man taking my black woman," he shot back.

"You don't have a black woman," I said to him. "As a matter of fact, you don't have a woman at all!"

"Michael," Mother snapped. "Boom Boom is a guest in our home."

"And so is Eddie," I did not hesitate to remind them all.

"Michael, watch your tone with your mother," Bula said sternly.

"Great potato salad," Eddie added, which made everyone at the table, including myself, turn and look at him.

"What about all the black men who date white women?" I couldn't help but go there. "No one has a problem with that, right? Except of course the black woman. The black man isn't boasting of his black woman when he's racing around town trying to get in the white woman's panties."

"I will not tolerate this kind of talk in my home," Mother said, outraged.

"To be honest, I've never dated an African American woman before," Eddie said. "The opportunity never presented itself. But the day I saw Michael, I felt electricity. Her smile took my breath away. I could literally feel myself succumb to her beauty and grace. There were plenty of other women around the day I met Michael, but she was special. She wasn't black or white, rich or poor, educated or uneducated. She wasn't someone to win or conquer. What I adored most about her was quite simple. She was alive."

Eddie then turned to my mother. "If it would make you more comfortable, I could rub shoe polish on my face and change my color. And I would be willing to do that if it would make you more comfortable, but I hope that you will simply allow me the honor of adoring your daughter as much as you have done all of her life . . . in spite of my color."

Fat ass Bula and Boom Boom were speechless.

Mother was taken back.

And the gossip queen did something totally unexpected. She reached across the table and slowly extended her hand to Eddie. And when Eddie accepted, she said, "Welcome to the family."

After Bula and Boom Boom left, Drunetta pulled Eddie to the family room to watch *Who Wants to Be a Millionaire?* It looked like Eddie had won over at least *one* other person besides me.

I helped Mother in the kitchen with dishes and did damage control. Mother was sulking. It was a very specific *I am truly disappointed in your taste in men* kind of sulking. She was waiting on me to apologize for my behavior and for embarrassing her by bringing a white man to the dinner table. She didn't say that, but then again she didn't have to. Daughters can read their mother's minds and vice versa.

She wouldn't be content until I took off my heels and jumped in her kitchen sink and did the backstroke around dirty suds in apology. She was so accustomed to being catered to, but today I had no immediate plans to bend, yield, apologize, or take back the choice that I made to date Eddie.

"What's on your mind?" I asked.

"I'd rather not discuss it," she said in that dull drum voice, doing it only the way she could do it.

"Mother . . ."

"I wish dinner would have been nicer," she said, racing laps around half-truths.

"And Eddie would have been *darker*," I replied sitting the whole truth on top of the counter. Mother's eyes jumped, and her shoulders rose in defense.

"Watch yourself," she warned.

"He's a great guy, Mother. Drunetta can see that. Why can't you?"

"Cause Drunetta's a fool sometimes," she scowled.

"Mother, Eddie is a good man. Can't you feel his goodness?"

"It's not his color that's bothering me," she snapped.

"Then what?" I asked.

"For starters," she said in her overly righteous voice, "he's not a Christian."

"He believes in God," I defended. "I'm pretty sure he does . . ."

She shot me an evil eye.

"He's not successful."

"He works."

"He's not good husband material."

"I can mold him."

"Are you really that naive, Michael?"

"Well, maybe living here twenty-nine years has done me some injustice," I said in retaliation for not being able to defend him good enough.

"Be careful," she warned, turning her back to me. Oh boy, I knew what that meant—be careful of her and be careful of Eddie. The only thing I didn't know was who was I to be more careful of, her or him.

"What would your father say if he were here?" she said, pricking me in places I thought had gone numb.

"Mother, what if Jesus were sitting at the table with us tonight? Don't you think Jesus would be more open-minded to Eddie?"

She gave a look but not a reply. She jumped out of that conversation and into another one.

"What happened to that nice young man, Sky? Why can't you be with him?"

"He doesn't want to be with me, Ma . . . He's not feeling me like that."

"It takes time to develop those kind of feelings," she said.

"Mother, I have known Sky for years. He's not feeling me."

"Well . . . maybe you should start feeling him!" she snapped.

Mother, are you on medication? I wanted to ask.

"He's so right for you," she said.

"Just because he's a black man doesn't mean he's the *right* man for me."

"You two look so good together. You care about him. He cares about you. He has steady work. He can take care of you and babies. He's responsible. This guy seems like a big flake!"

"Eddie's progressive, and he likes change. It doesn't mean he's a flake. . . . He's just feeling his way around."

"And is he feeling his way around you, too?" she asked in a low, direct tone. My mother had never spoken to me about things of a fleshy nature between men and women. Discussions centering on sex were off-limits. And if she continued down this line of questioning, I was probably going to throw up.

"Mother," I started, "you're scaring me."

"I thought so." She turned her back on me for the second time and walked away.

She had angered and embarrassed me tonight, but now she had hurt me. I grabbed my purse and stood in the doorway.

"Eddie, I'm ready," I called.

He entered with Drunetta hanging off his heels like a puppy chasing a bone. *Good Lord.*

"Good night," said Eddie to Mother. "And thank you for dinner."

"Good night," Drunetta said. "See you, Michael," she mumbled with much less enthusiasm.

"See you," I replied arrogantly. After all, she was pushing up on *my* man. Oh yeah, finally my mother chimed in offering a slow response to Eddie's farewell. "Good night," she said to him not skipping a beat from scrubbing dishes in the sink. She didn't even bother to look up.

I left that night without saying good-bye to my mother.

I didn't utter a word about the evening and neither did Eddie. These were the conditions for what seemed like the better part of the drive back home. I didn't even speak up when he took a wrong turn and headed in the opposite direction from my house. Eventually, we'll end up somewhere, I presumed. And eventually we did.

He pulled onto a dimly lit street, neatly lined with tiny row houses. We rolled down the block and made a sharp left into a circular drive. *Oh, now this is cute.* Here lies another example of a man who cannot accept his navigational inadequacies.

"Eddie, you took a wrong turn three miles ago," I said frustrated.

"No, I didn't," he said turning off the car. "I don't take wrong turns." Then the keys came out of the ignition and his behind came out of the seat. "You gonna sit there all night or are you actually going to get out and see where I live?"

"Oh. My bad," I said, easing out of the car, trying to disguise shock and disorientation for fatigue. The men I date never bring me to their homes. And that could be largely due to the fact that my presence would upset their wife, children, and the old lady (mother-in-law) living in the back room.

"You live here?" I asked, slow dancing up the cobblestone drive. "I thought you were homeless."

"Why did you think I was homeless?" he asked, fumbling with the keys.

"Because I've never seen your house before."

He stepped back, cocked his head to the side, and took in an expanded view of the house. "Well, it's a little bulky to carry around on top of the Jeep."

I laughed.

I had to.

And it wasn't because he was terribly funny or witty. I laughed because I could feel myself falling so hard. So here I stood, on his doorstep in tight black pants and studded sandals, straddling the fence somewhere between a crush and a fatal attraction.

Keep me forever, I wanted to say. Keep me when I'm down with the flu and funny bumps are growing on the back of my tongue from infection. Keep me when my press-and-curl starts to wear out around the edges. Keep me even when my legs aren't shaved and I have a premenstrual breakout on my chin and bloat in my belly. Keep me when the white of my teeth fades to a hollow yellow and the darkness of my hair turns to a taunting gray. Keep me when I'm not as beautiful as I look right now, framed under the light of the moon. Keep me after my ass outgrows the nifty size five I am wearing today and my breasts can no longer stand at attention on their own. Keep me when. Keep me *then.*

This wasn't a movie, but I sure felt like a movie star when he opened the door and I walked inside. The interior was simple, but stylish. Subtle, yet impressionable. As he led me by the hand like a tour guide through a foreign city, I was able to ascertain that his world was quaint, cozy, and comfortable. It resembled sane and somewhat normal.

I cherished that feeling and the moment I stepped inside I knew I *never* wanted to leave. The living area housed an oversized sofa and chair that sat on top of a hardwood floor. The dining room and kitchen were tiny; probably had enough room for two people and one dinner plate.

The bathroom was decorated in dark colors, boring and manly. But I did catch the porno stash on the back of the toilet. And by the looks of things he was a porno junkie (read between the lines: habitual slave of masturbation), like me.

My tour of his home continued where he led me to the back room. My heart was racing so fast I thought it would do a somersault and emerge flying through my chest.

"What's behind door number three?" I asked, laughing, trying to make a joke lest I pass out right on top of the pinewood.

He didn't respond, just slowly opened the door and pulled me into his world.

19

LIQUID

I was speechless.

This room was dimensionless.

Timeless.

Breathless.

Weightless, but all the while consuming. The room was absent of light but present with darkness. When I looked up I could see myriads of stars because Eddie had cut the roof off and replaced it with glass.

Papa, can you see me? I almost asked out loud. *Can you see your little girl way down here?*

The room was angled by hundreds of mirrors that served no purpose other than distraction. Some were leaning, while others were bending, and yet still others chose to spiral. Some saluted while others offered unkindness with their reflection. Eddie watched me watch the room that was so alive it watched me back.

"I spent my life savings to build this room," he said. "This is my illusion."

"You spent your life savings on an illusion?" I asked.

"Yes," he smiled proudly.

Damn, maybe Mama was right. Maybe Eddie was a flake.

"Why?" I wanted to know.

"Why not?" posing question to question.

"What do you do in here?" I turned to ask him, but just like that, he was gone.

Disappeared.

Blown away.

Withdrawn.

Creepy.

"Eddie," I called to him with urgency. *This weird mother-you-know-what better quit playing.* "Eddie, you're scaring me."

"Don't be scared," he said, suddenly showing up behind me. I tried to grab his arms, but my hands sliced through his body, which was only a reflection of the real thing. The image hastily withdrew and disappeared.

"It's just an illusion," he said appearing in front of me. I jumped, screamed, and that illusion, too, faded from my presence.

"It's not real," he said showing up to my left, then to my right. "Is perception our reality or reality our perception?" he asked, appearing in front of me again. I quickly turned away from what I believed to be his reflection, and just as I did he pulled on my hand and disappeared.

I screamed, again.

Okay.

This demented game of cat-and-mouse had lost its charm

and the next time he appeared in breathing, living flesh, I was going to sock him.

"Can you see an illusion?" he asked, now on top of the ceiling. "Or feel one?" In less than a blink, he suddenly appeared behind me, locking arms around my waist. He had come to me so smoothly that he sucked me up in the process. I didn't want to yield to his command or bend to his desire, but I did because I couldn't help myself. I couldn't help myself because he was beautiful and because he was on time. I couldn't help myself because he was what I wanted, needed, prayed for, and waited on. I couldn't help myself because he had taken time to polish the rust off my heart. I couldn't help myself because he was more than just a pretty boy in a nicely wrapped package. He was a package worth opening, and so I stripped him down to nothing.

And naked.

Oh, God, naked.

The angled mirrors boasted of magnificent nakedness. His clothes were gone and so were mine. Mine had fizzled under the weight of heavy hands and pounding hearts as he fondled the side of my neck, teasing, pleasing, demanding, and giving much more to me than I could ever repay.

His body was a just representation of time well spent pumping iron. I couldn't help but pour my flesh around him in an embrace so intense it could have been easily interpreted as strangulation.

"Oh, God," I exasperated as he twisted me toward a mirror

and pushed my beating heart against it. He encompassed me from behind, mounting his muscle upon my back. He rubbed and gripped, explored and claimed my Magic Kingdom for himself. He declared himself conqueror and king, making primitive sounds that I didn't understand.

"You feel so good," I think he whispered. But I couldn't be sure if that's what he said because I had temporarily gone deaf. The overstimulation of my nervous system was slowly causing my chambers to shut down one by one lest I fall on top of a cardiac arrest and die right here, smashed against a pillar of glass in a room of illusion. And that's not a pretty way to die.

"I can't breathe," I think I said.

Or maybe it was, "I'm dying."

My eyes crossed one another and all I could see was an onslaught of delusional images of him and me making love in contorted mirrors. From every angle I watched us make love. I counted the reps of his rocking hips working it out behind me. I searched with my eyes for places on the floor for our sweat to fall upon me, behind me, around me, and inside me.

"I crave you," I whispered. "I *crave* you . . ."

Come.

Come.

Come.

And come again, I think I said.

Then I fell onto the floor and passed out.

———

Till morning.

When I awoke I was lying in his bed. He was there, too, so it wasn't awkward. No. I lied. It was awkward, almost clumsy and inverted, too. I was lying in the evidence of what had happened the night before, and it was sticking to me like glue. It was pulling, gnawing, and guiding me to the uneasy chair, a swiveled lap of confusion, self-doubt, and regret.

I wasn't sure about any of this.

Most of us never are.

I turned away from him and buried my head under the covers. Even though we had waited a couple of months to consummate the relationship, I still couldn't help but wonder if it had happened too soon. But I couldn't take it back now even if I wanted to. And neither could he. So here goes another calculated risk taken on a longshot that this one might sustain itself under the weight of predestined damnation.

He was slowly waking, winding, twisting, and stretching. And I, I lay there like a cement doll. He scooted behind me and wrapped himself around me, kissing the curve of my back all the way down to the bottom.

"Good morning," he whispered.

"Morning," I said, easing myself out of hysteria.

So, he doesn't hate me.

Yet.

"Did you sleep well?" he asked.

"Yes," I replied turning over. "Did you?"

"Oh, yeah," he said, dramatically turning over onto his back.

Okay.

That was a good sign. And he's not escorting me out to the trash with the used condoms. Another good sign.

He rested his arms behind his head while he stared at the ceiling. His expression was so intense that for a moment, I, too, almost looked upward to see what he was looking at. But I already knew that there was nothing on the ceiling but whatever image he had in his head.

I climbed on top of him and felt engorgement.

His and mine.

Mine and his.

It was a pulsing surge of electricity flowing from my kingdom to his country so intensely it could barely be contained. I pulled back the covers and did my thing. Did my thing. And did my thing some more until there was nothing left to do except *recover*.

Distraction descended without warning when suddenly my pager, which had been going off the past hour, started up again. The same number kept arriving on my screen, but this time, the number came with urgency: 911.

"It's a 911 page," I said to Eddie, like he really cared. "Can I use your phone?"

"Sure," he said, surrendering his cordless.

I dialed, not expecting much at all till the caller on the other end said frantically, "Hello!"

"This is Michael . . . did someone—" I had begun to ask but was answered before I asked. And then I was on my way.

Eddie said nothing and neither did I.

I was scared.

I didn't want to take him with me but my car was at my house and I didn't have time to waste on a drop-off/pickup. I was a nervous wreck contemplating the unanswerable: do I tell him the truth or not? Our relationship is so new and fragile, is he ready for the less than pretty part of my world?

"Turn here," I directed.

"Left here."

"Right here."

As we descended deeper into the hood, home values fell like pigeon droppings. Emaciated crackheads were like streetlights, one on every corner. Trick hos were hustling customers for cash and hits off the pipe. The homeless faded into background scenery, making this street ripe material for a documentary on the long-range effects of single parenting and heroin addiction. Juveniles aspiring to be delinquents congregated by the hundreds to display their partiality for sign language, throwing gang signs to the enemy.

Turn the car around, I wanted say but couldn't. We had to go deeper. And in a neighborhood like this, a white man and a black woman could only be characterized as one thing; an eyesore. I wished he had tinted windows or at the very least a bulletproof vest in the glove compartment.

"You're definitely not in Kansas anymore, Dorothy," I said to Eddie.

"No shit," was his only reply.

I begged Eddie to stay in the car because there was no reason he should be a witness to this madness. I banged on the splintered door and the keeper let me in. She always called me when hell broke lose. And for all intents and purposes, hell had broken and suspended itself on the hind legs of imminent destruction.

The keeper was a wafer-thin black woman wearing a do-rag and horn-rimmed glasses. She looked more like a librarian and less like the rebel she was. Being a keeper was a hard job, a tough calling. Keepers ran unauthorized drug rehab programs across the city called safe houses. I use the word *unauthorized* because safe houses were not approved by the government to assist in the detoxification of drug addicts. But their role was vital, as they were the last stop for desperate addicts. It was their final link to the living and the only bridge separating them from the dead. Safe houses operated on the down low and they all shared a universal theme, which hung from the door upon entry. It read; "This Establishment Is Not County, State, or Your Mama Approved."

The safe house was a tough place. And there were only two ways to emerge from a safe house: clean or dead. The patients who survived treatment were usually cured forever, and those too weak to get through the unconventional, non-FDA-approved therapy, died.

No one knew for certain the number of safe houses in operation, nor what actually went on at the treatment center, but upon admittance, each patient received an angel of mercy visit. And that's where I came in. I served as a volunteer for the obscure program.

I became an angel of mercy a few years ago because I believed one person could make a difference. And I believed the down-trodden could benefit from the compassion I dumped on losers. It was also a great excuse to get me out of serving turkey dinners to the hypocrites in big hats and flower dresses resembling small tents at Mother's church. This was my contribution to humanity.

It was a good deed in one hand and a bad deed in the other because I knew the treatment was illegal. Safe houses took in demons off the streets and gave them one more chance at redemption. And who was in a position to judge that? Certainly not me.

When I entered the room, I found a new recruit in con-straints with her head lowered. She was definitely in need of an angel. Her shirt was off and her breasts were dangling on air. I had seen a little of this and a lot of that through the years, but nothing prepared me for this. When she looked upward our eyes locked and I felt a surge of pain shoot through me. I turned away for a beat and grabbed the wall to catch my footing.

"Molly Wood," I said quietly. "Oh, Molly Wood."

After we left, Eddie couldn't take his eyes off me. He was wait-ing for the dissertation on what had just occurred, but I wasn't giving up the juice. He extended a gentle, one-arm embrace from the other side of the Jeep. My cheeks were stained with many tears and my eyes were swollen, partly cloudy.

"What just happened back there?" asked Eddie, driving like a bat out of hell trying to get out of the ghetto before sunset.

"I don't want to talk about it," I said.

"Is this something that I should be worried about?" he asked.

No.

And yes.

Disintegration of a society and the walking death of the human spirit are things we should all be concerned about. On a macro level, it's just too damn hard to weep for every soul who succumbs. On a micro level, one person can change the world.

"No," I replied. "It's nothing for you to worry about."

"Can we talk about it?"

"No."

"Do you trust me?" he asked.

"Define trust," I answered.

Sticky silence stuck to both of us for a while.

"Do you have trust issues?" he asked.

"What?"

"Do you have trust issues?" he asked again, like I didn't hear him the first time.

"This is not about trust," I snapped.

"That's exactly what this is about."

"I don't want to talk about it."

"Okay. We don't have to, but you should seriously consider therapy to address your issues," he inserted before ejecting from the conversation.

I wanted to slug him for that last comment.

But I didn't.

And the only reason I didn't was because "therapy" had taught me how to redirect my anger.

After witnessing Molly's lockdown in the safe house, my spirits were wishing-well deep. Molly Wood was never going to get it right. Her issues seemed too big for anyone to save her.

I sat on the edge of Eddie's bed in the dark with my body facing toward blackness and no answers. The window was half open and Mother Nature was spilling hot air onto the bed. I probably should have gone home, but he didn't offer to drive and I didn't ask to go.

"Where are you?" he called to me from the opposite end of the bed.

"I'm not here," I replied half kidding, half not.

"Then *where* are you?" he asked again.

"I don't know . . ."

He eased his way to the bed and sat down beside me. He pulled out a book and began reading me a story. It wasn't just *any* story, it was the story of Goldilocks.

"Why do you have that book?" I said abruptly. At first I was scared. I had this eerie feeling that Papa sent Eddie to me in exchange for his absence. Like he was trying to make it up to me, being gone and dead all at the same time.

"Picked it up at a garage sale," he casually replied. "You said it was one of your favorites, right?" When I saw Eddie wasn't making a big deal over it, I just assumed that maybe I was reading too much into the situation, as usual. I mean damn, it wasn't as if Eddie was sent here to seal up all the cracks of my childhood.

"Yeah," I responded slowly. "It's one of my favorites."

As he began to read I closed my eyes and took in the sooth-ing sound of his voice as he impersonated both the humans and the bears. I could feel tears in the background trying to push their way to the foreground, but I refused to allow them entry.

I missed Papa so much. I missed him much more than I allowed myself room to miss him.

I opened my eyes and watched Eddie read. The words left him, almost in slow motion, as I fell deeper into him.

"Come here," I commanded, pulling him closer to me.

He obeyed, but hesitated to the point where I could sense his apprehension.

"What's wrong?" I asked.

He looked at me sharply, then turned away before respond-ing. "Nothing." But I didn't believe him.

"Eddie?" I called to him.

"Everything's okay," he said trying to convince himself more than I was actually convinced.

"Are you scared?" I asked.

"A little nervous," he finally admitted after a long pause in the conversation.

"About?"

"You."

"I don't understand," I replied.

"I don't want to hurt you," he said.

I pulled him close and whispered gently into his ear, "Then don't."

We didn't say anything else after that, but I should have known that was the beginning of his exodus. But silly me, just because his body was still there, which by the way he wrapped around me like finely tuned machinery, I assumed so was the rest of him.

Oh, Michael Morgan when will you ever learn?

I used two fingers to stroke his cheeks, then one tongue to lick his lips. I brushed my face against his and took note of our differences. His lips felt different than mine, a little softer perhaps, but not by much. His lips were thinner, a littler smaller, but again not by much. His mouth slightly parted and extended a nonverbal invitation for my tongue to enter. And I did, enter that is, slowly, feeling my way around his teeth and gums. A gentle journey ensued, a thorough exploration of his mouth against mine, mine against his. I could taste him so well and it was a taste worth taking in retrospect. For a moment, we were like cannibals feasting on one another for comfort.

Are you my comfort food?

"Knowing there is language where there are no words, knowing there is music where there is no sound, knowing there is movement where bodies lay still . . . that's my definition of trust," he said.

"Wow," I said, deeply impressed.

"I know," he said interrupting the flow. "I was impressed, too, when I read it in *Reader's Digest*."

I rolled my eyes, adding "so much for originality," as I turned over onto my back and laughed out loud. I lay there for a moment before he scooped me up into his body. His hands were like wings, scanning the full length of me and mine. His skin, a giant organ all its own, delivered elegance and eloquence, bruising me with his scent, up and down, in and out, on and on. When he finally entered me, I gasped relief and desperation all in the same exhale. My legs parted and our bodies became a singular unit. And up until the moment he closed his eyes and drifted from consciousness, we were liquid, he and I.

20

EBB 'N' FLOW

One minute I'm lying in his arms and eternity is almost possible. The next moment I'm back in my own bed, the one where I wake up alone each day grasping for straws and a profound acceptance of the truth. Eternity isn't possible—it's not even plausible. No matter how legit the relationship seems, I still can't help but wonder if the whole thing is nothing more than a ploy to utilize my body for sexual gratification.

I was uneasy about Eddie's apprehension from the night before. When a guy says he doesn't want to "hurt you," get the Band-Aids ready, because more than likely a heart is about to break, and I guarantee it won't be *his*. At least that's been my experience from the past. Too much of a past. Too many fragmented moments in my life, still frames I tried to string together. They were frames that didn't quite tell the story in its entirety because the picture got fuzzy when the guy disappeared. I have struggled to make sense of the disappearing acts of men, which has only served to make me distrustful of them. So, no matter how sincere Eddie appears when professing "like of me," I still can't help but believe he is a pathological liar.

No matter how he seemed to adore me, I still can't stop asking, "Who else is he sleeping with besides me?" And more important, "When, oh, when is he leaving?"

My foot landed on Mabel's "unwelcome mat." When she opened the door I immediately displayed a large bucket of hot wings and a jumbo-sized box of toothpicks.

"You must be desperate today," she huffed.

"Not really," I grinned.

"Desperate," she confirmed opening the door, allowing me to enter without a hassle or a strip down. Mabel looked exhausted, like she had wrestled a crocodile all night. She slowly hobbled to a chair and fell back into it, breathless.

"Are you okay?" I asked.

"I've seen better days," she mumbled.

Suddenly, I felt a wave of sympathy for Mabel. She was alone. Never married. She bore no children. Both parents, African immigrants, were dead. I had often wandered if she ever saw that her own future would be such a lonely one.

I tried to give her the chicken wings, but she motioned for me to set them down on the table instead.

What? Mabel's not hungry? Somebody better dial 911.

"Are you up for this today?" I asked.

"That's not what you came here to ask," she snapped. *Uh-oh, time for the evil twin to emerge.* "You came here to ask me about *him*," she said.

"I came here to ask you about Eddie," I said.

"I don't need you tell me his name cause I see him clear as day!" she shouted. "So, you took up sleeping with the devil?"

Truth be told, I had slept with so many men I didn't know which devil Mabel was talking about. As far as I was concerned they were *all* devils.

"You laid down with him and filled yourself with his pollutants!" she wailed.

"What?" I asked, slightly freaked.

"And still you are contaminated," she added.

Okay. So, I'm contaminated. I made a mental note and moved on. But before I could grasp her words, Mabel began groaning and writhing in her seat. Her body contorted, and she started singing a Negro spiritual in Swahili. Well, if that wasn't enough to shake up my nerves, I didn't know what was. I didn't know what the hell was going on, but an immediate exit became my highest priority. The crazy look in Mabel's red eyes would lead one to think that she, too, was sleeping with the devil, if not the devil herself.

"Good-bye," she howled.

I must have leapt ten feet out of my chair and straight out the door.

"Shit," I murmured looking through the peephole from the other side of safety. Maybe Molly Wood was right. Maybe Mabel was a crazy coot after all, hustling the neighbors for chicken wings and potato salad, toothpicks and malt liquor. Yeah, maybe Mabel was crazy. But then again maybe she *wasn't*.

———

Time has a clever way of incinerating our dreams and delivering flawed human beings from the exhausted wombs that tried so hard to keep them. Molly Wood was a perfect example of that as she battled the demons and the drugs simultaneously. By now her demons had grown to life-size replicas of a life not well lived at all.

I waited until I could stomach the smell before I went back to the safe house. Honestly, it was just too hard seeing Molly Wood depleted. You think it would have been a sight I would have gotten used to by now, but I just never did.

I found Molly out back on a step, staring at the ground and the sky. I came up behind her and sat down just like I did back in our elementary school days.

I sat without announcement or incident, but my entrance was quiet thunder.

Loud but soft.

It was a gentle reminder that no matter how alone Molly Wood felt she wasn't doing it entirely on her own. I brushed my shoulder against hers. It was my way of saying, "Hello."

Hello, she echoed by brushing back.

"How's life?" I asked with my eyes cast downward on the same ground that mesmerized her.

"And the beat goes on," she replied without enthusiasm.

"And on and on," I said, then asked, "How you doing in here?"

"Shitty."

"You're in a good place, Molly Wood," I reminded her.

"No one in rehab is in a *good* place," she scolded. "If I were in such a good place I wouldn't be in this shit hole—"

"This shit hole could save your life."

"You presume it's worth saving," she said matter of factly.

I looked at her, but didn't respond. Because I just didn't know what to say.

"Is it worth saving?" she wanted to know.

"You have to ask me that?" I asked.

"Just need to be reminded," she said.

There are certain questions in life that are unanswerable in words, only in love and action. I put my arms around Molly Wood and pulled her close to me. I pulled her close and kept her there for a long time.

Meanwhile, back at the ranch I had my own demons to contend with. My relationship with Eddie had begun to shift. Actually *shift* was a kind word—*crumble* at the seams was a more accurate depiction. A relationship that appeared to be carried on the wings of a rising star had quickly disintegrated into a burning meteorite plunging to the center of the earth, earmarked to take out babies and old people first. About a month into our "committed" relationship, Eddie started pulling away for "no apparent reason" and excuses become part of his daily routine.

I can't see you today because . . .

I can't stay longer because . . .

I didn't call you today because . . .

I didn't return your call because . . .

And I won't call you tomorrow because . . .

Our relationship had begun to feel like a frantic game of dodgeball.

I was shooting and missing.

He was ducking and dodging.

And all the while I did what drowning people do: fight harder and sink faster.

One day while he and I were on what felt like an obligatory lunch date on his end, I confronted him by asking, "What's going on with you?"

"We should take a break," he flat-out said. There wasn't even a pause or a beat before he blurted it out like that.

Whoa.

What the hell??

"We should take a break?" I repeated flabbergasted.

"Yeah," he replied quickly.

"Why?" I challenged.

"Because I've got a lot going on . . ."

"Like?" I persisted.

"Work shit."

"What's that got to do with us?"

"Not everything has something to do with *us*!" he snapped. "Why does the whole world have to revolve around *us*? This isn't about you, Michael! I just need to be alone for a while."

Well, damn.

And this is where I took a turn for the worse. It was an unsuspecting blow beneath the belt in the eleventh hour.

I can't lose him.

Oh God, I can't *lose* him.

"You mean we should break up," I restated.

"No, I mean we should take a break," he tried to clarify.

"Define break," I demanded.

"Pause the relationship."

"End the relationship?" I asked.

"I didn't use the word *end* . . ."

"If something doesn't go on . . . it ends . . ."

And of course he turned into a deaf-mute right about here.

"I don't want to take a break," I said with my arms crossed, trying to be cool. "If you want to bust a move, then break up with me. But I'm not taking a break. That's ridiculous," I said. "Are you breaking up with me, Eddie?"

He didn't say anything.

"Are you breaking up with me?"

Mr. Quick Lips remained silent.

"Eddie, you can't break up with me," I said like a wilting flower, so desperate for light and love. "And do you want to know why?"

"Why?" he asked with a giant sigh.

"Because you still haven't taught me how to ride a bike yet," I replied gently. "So there you go."

He nodded—didn't say a word just nodded.

I thought I had won because I called his bluff, and he cowered. But like I said before, life has a way of snatching our victories away and replacing them with defeat.

After lunch he drove me *straight* home. He pulled up to my

apartment and kept the car running. Suddenly, it felt less like a breezy afternoon and more like a judgment day. Someone had to make a move, take a stand, crush a heart, or break a spirit. And of the two of us, who had more to lose? Who would say something, anything? Who would yield or take the more humble position? Who would take a swing at peace? A stab at serenity? A shot at understanding? It all came down to one thing: Who needed who more? Who could walk away right now and not despair? And more important, who couldn't?

"Will you come in?" I asked, losing round one.

"I have to take care of some things," he said flatly.

Okay. Do I exit the car right now with a drop of dignity intact, or do I beg for reconciliation and watch my ego dissipate into nothingness?

It all boiled down to a very thin bottom line: Who was being pulled down the street, around the corner, and halfway across the world by the piercing blade of crave? And who wasn't?

I wanted to reach out and touch his hand or rub his shoulder or stroke his hair, but I couldn't. I wanted, no, I needed final confirmation that we would be okay. And even if we weren't okay right now, I needed to know that eventually we would be. I could feel my heart stirring, a nervous agitation.

"Will you call me later?" I asked, struggling on the threshold of collapse.

"Sure," he said.

I was on the verge of begging him to come inside, but a teaspoon of self-respect prevented that from happening. *Thank God.* So I got out of the Jeep, shut the door, and walked away—

Without looking back.

And there would be no kisses today.

No hugs.

No affection or admiration.

No special consideration of any kind.

God, this was tough. I felt as though I were dragging my heart on the bottom of my leather boots. I made it to my door with scrap marks on the tender parts as he sped away without regard for the bruised feelings I had spilled along the way.

A break? I kept repeating in my mind.

Pause in the relationship?

I walked into my apartment at four o'clock in the afternoon and retired for the evening. I popped a Tylenol with codeine to quiet the conversation in my head. Before drifting off my brain processed a final thought, which my heart didn't hesitate to remind me of: one minute I'm lying in his arms and eternity is almost possible. The next moment I'm back in my own bed, the one where I wake up alone each day grasping at straws and a profound acceptance of the truth. Eternity isn't possible, it's not even plausible. And such is the ebb 'n' flow of our lives.

21

TWO DANCES, ONE PAIR OF LEGS

I had unplugged the phone before I went to bed yesterday lest I wake up every hour checking to see if I had missed a call that would never come. And I would have, don't you know? I would have forced myself awake to check for messages, crunched in half, hanging off the side of the bed with blurred vision searching for a blinking message light and an apology. And I would have plunged to the depths when I saw there was nothing to see. I replayed yesterday's events frame by frame searching for a happy ending. And that, too, never came.

"Will you call me later?"

"Sure . . ."

And

"Sure . . ."

And "Sure?" I think he said.

Later never came.

Ambiguity is the wine of the insane, and I caught myself becoming intoxicated on its fumes. What the hell happened? Was I no longer lovable? And worthy? A decent companion?

Did he kick me to the curb without a good-bye? The labor of questions without the delivery of answers only enhanced my dementia.

"Wrong" my coworker Timm said. "You should have never insisted on a commitment from the guy."

"Why?" I asked, sulking over a dead client's head.

"Because he wasn't ready," Timm said. "Obviously."

"So he's gone?" I asked.

And no answer came from the peanut gallery.

My gaze lowered to the body I was working on. It was the corpse of a thirty-three-year-old Asian woman named Luci. She had expired the night before. The cause of her demise was stomach cancer. Luci was a beautiful corpse, which indicated that her death was a swift one. I had worked on a number of cancer deaths through the years and knew all too well the emaciation of the disease. But Luci was different. She still had a substantial amount of meat on her bone and her skeleton had not yet been introduced to the other side of her body, indicating her cancer was acute, aggressive.

Luci was manicured and well groomed. It appeared that just prior to her departure she had her nails done. I found this morbid pastime, looking at the dead to ascertain tiny details of their lives, an art form.

Luci had a peaceful resolve about dying, and I identified that through the partial smile she wore on her face. Effortlessly, I was able to absorb a plethora of information about the deceased. But there would always be remnants of a past that would remain privy to the dead and those who knew them best.

Did Luci ever love someone with all of her heart? And was he kind enough to return the favor? Did her eggs yield human beings in the form of children? I pondered such absurdities about all of the corpses who were delivered to our doorstep by the men in white vans who discarded of the dead for a living.

I was having a difficult time preparing Luci for viewing. Her mouth kept opening, common among the dead, so I gathered my needle and thread to shut it. I applied superglue to open eyes and brittle hands that refused to hold one other. Luci's face had started to sink so I gave it a lift, implanting fillers in the jaw area. Unfortunately, bones had to be broken to lay her properly.

When it was time for makeup and hair, I wanted to do something different for Luci, something special.

"Special?!" screamed Mr. Tucker. "You mean to tell me you did that on purpose?" Okay. It was time to meet Howell Tucker, owner of Tucker Funeral Home. I could write an animated editorial on everything from this man's essence to his overgrown toenails, but I won't. The pictorial speaks for itself.

Forty-nine years old.

Five feet, six inches tall.

Short-man complex.

Third-generation mortician.

His signature was his comb-over and the blue pinstripe suite that he wore every *other* day.

His temper was ruthless, his ethics questionable.

His coffins were exorbitant and his limos raggedy. And with the exception of Timm and myself, it was difficult to distinguish between the staff who prepared the dead and the actual dead themselves. And the only reason I chose to work for this god-awful man was because I was complacent about my career. I was blasé, getting "phat" off the numbness of a consistent paycheck.

"I thought she was beautiful," I said, defending my work.

"Beautiful? A conservative Asian woman from a Buddhist family laid to rest in hot-pink lipstick, silver eye shadow, and six-inch lashes! Have you gone completely mad!"

"I felt a vibe. I was trying to express my creativity."

"No! No! No! Around here, we don't follow creativity, we follow instructions! We put the dead away with dignity. Remember? That's our motto, say it with me, 'Putting the dead away with dignity.'"

"Mr. Tucker, my work is an expression of myself," I replied instead.

"If you want to express yourself, take a painting class! This is a place of business—my business—and around here we put the dead away with—"

"I got it, Mr. Tucker."

"Dignity!" he finished. "Putting the dead away with dignity," he chanted dancing around like one of Santa's elves. "Putting the dead away with dignity."

I exited, leaving this idiot to the embrace of his own pep talk. I wanted to conclude our discussion by saying "See you later sucker," but office etiquette dictated something more along the lines of, "Thank you for your time."

What I really wanted to do was unzip my skin and step outside, but there would be no time for that. A guy had been killed in a sky-diving accident and his family was insistent upon an open casket service, which meant Timm and I, the dream weavers, had to work big miracles to make him look presentable. And this would be close to impossible because the man fell ten thousand feet with the only thing breaking his fall being his own ass. And while we worked feverishly to make him look human again, I overanalyzed how to piece myself back together as well. Yet somehow it all looked so sad, so bleak, for the dead man and for me.

"It's never going to happen for me," I said to Timm as I sulked.

"What?" he asked.

"Love."

"Here we go again," he said, offering flippancy to a critical situation.

"No, I'm serious . . ."

"You're so predictable," he said. "Why are you always so pushy with love?" he asked, which only pierced me.

"Because my eggs are dying!" I shouted. "Remember?"

"Oh, God," he said throwing up his hands.

"I always fall for the guys who will never fall for me," I said.

I was the one who arrived at the theater each night awaiting a grand production, but each time the curtain opened the stage was bare. And there I sat alone, under the weight of great distress that I was the only one who bothered to arrive. The seat beside me always remained painfully empty and perhaps this was largely due to my own desperation to find him.

Ladies and gentlemen, it was now official. The most recent dud I had fallen for (read between the lines: Eddie) was a no-show.

Two weeks had come and gone, riding on the belly of Eddie's absence. There would be no calls, no correspondence, no communication, or indulgences and no regard to the continuation of my ability or inability to breathe without him.

No exceptions.

What happens?

How do people just *change* like that?

How do people forget like that?

How do people walk away so easily unscathed?

Fourteen days would come and go, leaving me unable to distinguish between grief and grieving, with my greatest dilemma being how I would manage to console my emotions through the passing of yet another twenty-four hour period.

In the darkest of wee morning hours when the only choices that presented themselves demanded that I either breathe or suffocate to death, I sent the walls tumbling down and allowed the tears a release.

On one such night I found myself knocking on Sky's door, crawling into his bed for comfort. He had no better understanding of the situation than I did, and therefore was unable to offer little in the way of advice. The best he could do was swaddle me like an infant and absorb, if not my pain, then at least my tears. I wanted him to make the pain go away, but I couldn't inconvenience him by asking because that just wasn't his job. And it was apparent that he had been pulling double duty for years, as my imaginary lover and very real friend.

I couldn't ask him to put my tired mind at ease or quiet the incessant conversations of a desperate soul who wanted so badly to love and be loved in return.

I couldn't ask him to fill in the blanks where the words dropped off or put answers behind the question marks. I couldn't ask him to transform himself into "the one" and spare me from the rest of my life.

I grieved valuable, salty tears because the wounds were fresh and old, because love was almost obtained, just before it was lost for good. I was able to hold reality in my hand, but not tightly enough before it fled from my heart. And at the end of my journey, when I pulled the tape to measure the distance of this vast trip, imagine my dismay when I found I was still standing at the gate. And not even an inch could I count on the way to wherever the hell I was supposed to be going.

How did Eddie disappear into thin air, and where did he find the combination to erase his heart from feeling? Didn't he care about me or wonder what I had been up to these days? I wanted to know the answers, and I didn't want to guess at their accuracy.

And that was the only way I managed to justify rolling my car down his street. I was just going to "check things out." At least that was the lie I had told myself. A quick drive-by and an even quicker glance at his house to make sure it was still erect.

The first time I drove past the house, I could very well see it was standing and unmolested by the elements. His Jeep was parked in the driveway, so obviously he was home, but that wasn't enough. A glance didn't give me answers but only brought more questions. *If the house hadn't burned down why hadn't he called me?* This unanswered matter left me with no choice but to turn the car around and drive back down the street for a second look. I must say that I felt ridiculous when I threw the transmission into reverse, but that didn't stop me from rolling through again, half ducking as I passed the house, as if a headless driver wouldn't catch *everybody's* attention. Upon my arrival at the block's end, I was still not satisfied by what I had seen or not seen, so I turned around and rolled back through for a third time. But this time I stopped the car and turned off the motor.

"*Michael, go home,*" I said in a futile attempt to coax myself back to sanity. Go home and embrace the rest of your life. The one that knew you before you met *him* and the one that shall claim you long after he is gone. *Go home, Michael. Go home.* Wrap your arms around brittle dreams and a barely beating heart. *Go home, Michael. Go home.* And I was ready to obey this command until the door opened and out stepped a blonde with long legs and gargantuan breasts. She spilled out of his house, almost in slow motion, flowing down the driveway with Eddie close behind wagging his tail, panting his tongue.

I froze.

No, I died.

I could have fired up my engine and plowed them both into the pavement, but I paused so intelligence could catch up to emotion. And while I waited for that to happen I just stood there, stupefied, watching him open the car door, escorting this woman and her extra-large breasts inside. While observing their exchange, two dominant thoughts battled to the death inside my head, both searching for a superior position.

1) Exactly how many points would I get on my driving record for a hit-and-run leaving two Caucasian casualties dead in the middle of a quiet suburban neighborhood, and

2) How long did he suck on those giant jugs?

When she reached overhead to lower the convertible top of her sports car, I counted the diamonds on her finger. She was a flashy, glitzy, Las Vegas showgirl-type. Is *that* what turns him on? Fried blonde hair and store-bought breasts? I didn't rank any-where on that scale, not that I was trying to compare myself to a bimbo by any means.

He leaned against her car for a long time, laughing, chatting it up. He looked like he was walking on air, and I looked like I had just been rescued from a POW camp.

He looked content, I distraught.

And I hated him for that.

His eyes sparkled with each stroke of her hand to his face. *Hey! That's against the rules!* You're not supposed to sparkle over another girl. You're not supposed to be sharing your attention, affection, and charm. Why are you sharing? You're not allowed to take on side projects when I'm supposed to be your *primary* interest. We have a verbal contract, an oral obligation you, bastard. You made a promise. So I nudged you into the agreement, still, you stepped up and signed on the dotted line. How can you renege on that? You said we'd be together, exclusively, you and me. Not you, me, and that chick over there. What the hell is going on? Just because we haven't spoken in a few days doesn't give you the right to grope another woman's body. Does that justify you betraying my trust, destroying the contract, and torching my belief that once upon a time you were actually a decent human being? He nailed the coffin shut when I watched him tongue-kiss her for two minutes, thirteen seconds.

Anguish.

Pain.

Sorrow.

Hurt.

Betrayal.

And anger took turns stabbing me to death. How could he light a match and blow me up like that?

I hated him.

No sooner did the chick hit the gas then I hit the pavement, right out of my car and into his face.

"Who was that girl, Eddie?!" I screamed, sprinting toward him. His eyes did a dance against the back of his head. *Bewilderment becomes you.* All I needed was a two-by-four so I could bash him in the head as a parting gift.

"How could you?!" I screamed, pushing into his chest with my hands. "How could you?!"

"What are you doing here?" was all he could ask, throwing up his hands in disgust.

"I should be asking you the same thing!" I shouted, pointing in the direction of a barely visible sports car. "Who is she?" I demanded. "Are you fucking her, too?"

He took a long hard look at me, appraised the situation, sized it up in a snap, shook his head, turned around, and started walking to his front door.

"Eddie!" I called after him desperately.

He didn't answer.

"Eddie!" I shouted again, more desperate than before. I was about to crumble, and he just kept walking.

What was he doing?

Where was he going?

"Eddie!" I cried out again.

Is it over?

Are you done?

Is it over and are you done?

He turned his back on me like I never existed in his world.

As a child growing up, people always told me to "read between the lines." If I applied that advice to this situation, it yielded the obvious: "You are in this relationship by yourself." I had lost so much dignity up to this point there was nothing left to lose, except of course the hope that we would one day be together again, and I wasn't about to let that go. I was still drunk on champagne wishes of the way it *used* to be. I had solidified the high of falling in love, and I needed that feeling to keep breathing.

"Eddie!" I screamed. "Please, don't go! Please . . . let's just talk!"

I lost mega inches on my height that day. I diminished myself from five foot five to two foot one. The neighbors were staring out of their windows and passersby were clocking despair on my face.

"I loved you . . . Eddie . . . loved you so much," my final words tapered off to nothingness.

Oh, damn.

There is nothing more catastrophic than displaying your weakness to the masses.

Eddie slowed, then stopped and turned to face me. I couldn't translate the expression on his face, but I calculated it somewhere between resistance and surrender. I cautiously moved toward him, fearful that if I walked too fast, he would turn around and run like hell.

Would he stand there and wait for me to arrive, and if he did, what would he say when I got there? Would I forgive him for his indiscretions and would he forgive me for shedding my dignity like old, tired skin? When I finally arrived to where he stood it was instinctual for me to wrap myself around him. My arms reached for the thickest part of his body and held on. The moment I had him in my arms I felt relief from raging anxiety. He didn't respond for what seemed an eternity, and for a long, desperate beat, he just stood there with both arms holding firmly and tightly against his body. At first, he was resistant and I could feel him pull away as much as I could feel him leaning into me. Then, he finally released his energy and slowly wrapped his arms around me in an equally emotional embrace. We stood on the sidewalk holding each other, and when I could no longer hold it, I broke down and sobbed.

He walked me into his house and closed the door behind us. Aside from the neighbors getting a good show and me a good cry, there were obvious glitches in the relationship. How could we go on the same as we had before, now that so much had changed? So much was altered? Dirtied and destroyed? How could we continue? Probably the same way you do two dances with one pair of legs: *you can't.*

22

GIFT WRAPPED IN CHAINS

We were inseparable until he came.

After he dismounted, neither one of us knew what to say. He turned one way and I the other. Our backs faced one another, leaving us with no choice but to make love to the solitude we had chosen to create.

I couldn't ignore the blonde with legs that ran for days and breasts that spilled down to her knees. And he couldn't ignore that I begged him back on a public street while dissolving into a spineless beggar.

I couldn't ignore his disappearing act and the transparent ease with which he moved on to the next.

He couldn't ignore that I was probably in way too deep.

And I couldn't ignore that he *wasn't*.

This was my all-too-familiar mating dance—searching for love in places it did not exist and running away from places where it might actually be.

"I crave you more, don't I?" I said, facing my wall.

"Yes," he replied facing his.

"Do you love me, Eddie?" I asked.

There was nothing but silence and all truths were told within the confines of unspoken words.

"Wow," was all I could say, hard pressed against the facts.

"I care about you, Michael," he said as his voice tapered off into a whisper. And with this response I could hear a "but" coming all the way from Zimbabwe.

"But?"

"But I don't think it's going to work," he said rolling over.

"Why?" I asked wrestling tears, fighting them back.

"Too much, too soon," he said with finality.

I sat up in the bed and stared at the ceiling. "What does that mean?"

"I'm just not ready for this . . ."

"For what?" I asked for clarification so that I could know what I was dealing with.

"For this intensity . . . relationship . . . it's just too much . . ."

"Eddie, I don't understand . . ."

"There's nothing to understand," he said.

"Don't you feel the way I feel?" I asked with grave sincerity. Silence.

And that was my answer, which I already knew.

"I thought you liked me," I said bitterly.

"I do like you," he replied in a vaguely unconvincing tone.

"Then how could you sleep with another woman?"

"I like her, too . . ."

Ouch.

"So you sleep with *everyone* you like?"

"If it happens, it happens," he said with a snap.

"But you made a commitment to *me*. How could you sleep with someone after you made a commitment to me?" I said, trying to catch myself before I blew up.

"We broke up," he said flatly.

"You broke up," I said. "I was still in the relationship."

He sighed as frustration took over and he made a pathetic attempt to explain himself. "Okay. If two people are playing tennis and one person walks off the court, doesn't that mean the game is over?"

"This wasn't a game Eddie . . . at least it wasn't to me."

"Hypothetically speaking, Michael . . . come on . . ."

"No," I said, emotionless. "If one person leaves the court it doesn't necessarily mean the game is over!"

"What?" he asked, baffled.

"The person could be going to pee, Eddie. People walk off the court every day but they can always come back, right?" I was waiting for him to agree with me, but instead he turned away and buried himself in a pillow.

"What?" I asked, resting my face against his back.

"I wasn't coming back," he said.

Game over.

I could process departure, but what I could not process was how he could be with me one day and the next day walk through me as if I never existed at all. And even deeper, trade intimacy with someone else? Someone other than me? Someone who wasn't me? The last words he uttered chased me down the street on foot, making dents on top of my trunk as I drove blurry eyed, dazed, and confused. "See you around, Michael. See you around."

When a guy says, "See you around," what he's really saying is, "If by chance we meet as strangers on the street, perhaps I will acknowledge your existence, then again, perhaps I won't." What he's also saying is, "I'll never call again. I'll never care again, and I'll never come again."

See you around, sucker.

"See you around, dirt bag," I murmured. My anger overshadowed the hurt, which made the pain of the moment appear more bearable. My swelling temper provided cushioning for a bruised ego. And before it was all said and done, I would hate him and would also hate myself.

I hated him because he had come into my life with such cunning seduction that I was swept off my feet. He scouted my reservoirs, tore down my walls. I had no other choice at that point but to fall in love. And then he exited without warning and reason, providing no justification, compensation, or consolation for the rips and tears in my heart. And I hated myself because not only did I allow this to happen, but I begged him back for more. My esteem hit the toilet and floated there for a while, forcing me in front of a mirror painfully picking apart my blackness.

My nose was too big. Perhaps it was time to Europeanize the

broad structure. I had never given much thought to my nose, but when I compared myself to the tramp in Eddie's driveway, I realized it was much wider and less specific than hers was. And my lips, they were gigantic in comparison. Perhaps I should deflate them. And my cheeks? Did they even have bones to fill them in? I could see Blondie's cheekbones from a mile away, but mine looked to be filled with hot air and a whole lot of nothing. And my breasts, they weren't ballooned like hers. And my skin wasn't pale, and my hair was of another texture altogether. And my butt, well, okay, I win that one, but it didn't matter because perhaps when Eddie looked into my eyes he couldn't appreciate my beauty as it was, only as he wished it to be.

I was second-guessing myself right out of existence, and this led me to ponder whether blacks and whites should mix together at all on a romantic level. Maybe it just didn't fit, didn't jive, didn't blend. Maybe ebony and ivory only worked for Paul McCartney and Stevie Wonder. And maybe it was easier to go through life pondering what would never be instead of dealing with all that truly was.

"I'm going to get my nose fixed," I confided in Molly Wood as we sat on the back porch of the safe house. Molly was doing well in recovery, having passed round one of detoxification. I wanted to be supportive of her recovery but found myself tilting against the weight of my own issues, a humble slave to self-absorption once again.

"Is your nose broken?" she asked.

"It doesn't look right," I confessed, swatting gnats away from my face.

"But is it broken?" she asked again, paying more attention to her own reflection in a side window than to my nose. Molly was also a lifetime member in the club of self-absorption.

"No, it's not broken," I snapped, hoping my unpleasant tone would be worthy of eye contact. But it wasn't.

"Then don't fix it. You're beautiful just the way you are," she said plucking her eyebrows.

"I don't feel beautiful, Molly."

"Beauty's an inside job," she said.

Oh, this from the world's most narcissistic agent.

"Who says?" I challenged.

"Ugly people," she replied without conscience.

I laughed for a moment. It was nice to know that my face was still willing to turn in the direction of a smile, but it wouldn't last for long because the pain returned like a swift boomerang exacting justice for a crime I didn't commit.

"Why can't I let him go?"

"Because there's no one else to replace him with."

"He was so sweet when I first met him. How could he change like that?"

"He didn't change," Molly said, lighting a cigarette. She still hadn't managed to kick the smoking habit yet. "You're just seeing the real him for the first time. The bastard's true colors are glowing."

"Molly, he was *so* into me . . ."

"They usually are . . . in the beginning."

"What happened?" I asked.

"The pussy got old," she said without flinching.

Another recovering addict overheard our conversation and took it upon herself to join in. "When the pussy gets old you can forget it, girl," the other crackhead said. "You have to keep your man entertained if you want to keep him."

"We weren't together long enough for anything to get old," I said defensively.

"Haven't you heard of the three-times rule?" the other crack addict asked.

"No."

"Never have sex three times in the same position. It'll kill any relationship. Even the most stable relationships are destroyed when there's a violation of the three-time rule," Molly said with conviction.

"What?" I asked in disbelief. "That's the most ridiculous thing I've ever heard! There are only so many positions—"

"You see that?" Molly's friend accused. "That's why she lost her man!"

Molly and her crack buddy started laughing. They laughed as if it were any other day and any other day I wouldn't have minded. But today, I did mind and their laughter felt like infectious fungus, unpleasant.

"Okay," I said entertaining their madness as if it could *possibly* be true. "How many positions are there?"

"It's infinite, baby," said Molly.

"Yeah girl, it's—it's . . . whatever that word she used," said the other girl.

After I realized that I was taking these girls seriously, I couldn't help but shake myself back to the real world. "There's no such thing as infinite sexual positions," I said, hoping to clarify things for both idiots.

"We've counted them, bitch," the agitated junkie said.

"Yeah . . . she's counted them, honey bunny," Molly said.

Molly and the junkie continued to take turns perpetrating madness while I took my own turn to reflect on the obvious. I had forgotten one very important flaw to the three-time theory: *The bitches who wrote the theory were on crack.*

Case closed.

Mr. Tucker had eaten garlic for lunch. I don't mind garlic in its original form, however I didn't care for it much when rolled on the edge of a bitter tongue. A tongue that bruised me to death with insults because it could not comprehend my creativity nor understand the way I chose to lay the dead to rest.

"This is blasphemous!" he ranted, "and inexcusable!"

Harold Knott, my latest client, had been laid to rest wearing a toupee. His children hated the presentation and had gone to Tucker to complain. They said their father looked unnatural wearing the hair. My defense, "Of course he looked unnatural. He was *dead*."

Knott had lost most of his hair to old age and the balance to chemotherapy. I had chosen a wig for the old man for one simple reason: his wife had always loved his hair. And even though I wasn't in a position to play God and take away her pain, I was in a position to weave a dream or two and put an authentic smile on her face at the service, which, by the way, never happened.

"Sweet Jesus! You are going to run me straight out of business!" Tucker shouted as he strutted around his oval office in a tan suit because the pinstriped polyester had retired for the afternoon. "This is *my* funeral home. I make the rules and instigate the policies . . ."

Tucker kept talking, but I stopped listening, so I really don't know what else he said. As a matter of fact, there were only two things at that point that I did know: 1) my heart ached mercilessly for Eddie, and 2) this job was interfering with my personal life. So the next morning I called in sick and allowed the infamous prick Tucker to figure out how to bury the dead without me.

I really missed Mabel and needed her services more than ever. And if she weren't stone out of her mind, I would have knocked on her door with chicken wings and malt liquor in hand. But since she *was* stone out of her mind, the best I could do was seek advice from the usual people. You know, the same people everyone else consults when their life is in crisis, those who have no flipping idea what the hell is going on, and they speak mostly because they like the smell of their own breath and not because they actually have something of *value* to say.

"That's how men are," someone said.

"Men ain't no good," someone else said.

"You can't make him want to be with you," said some guy.

"He doesn't deserve you," said somebody I didn't know well.

"You deserve better," said somebody I don't know at all.

"Just move on," said Mother. Yes, I broke down and told my mother. And even though she wasn't entirely over her tantrum, she had a lovely contribution to make when she said, "Next!"

"There's more fish in the sea," said the shrink as I parted with my last seventy-five bucks.

By the time night threw its blanket over the sun my mouth was tired and dry. I was exhausted and depressed. Countless hours of conversation about Eddie had drained my spirit. I had consulted with more people than the president. I had spoken to old friends, new friends, strangers, and enemies seeking advice, direction, and answers that could only come from Eddie himself.

Desperation is a bargaining tool of the insane. How else could I justify asking people who had never even met Eddie to peel off his exterior and define his inner chambers? I was asking people who didn't know him to read his heart and summarize his intentions with accuracy.

"Is he going to call again?" I asked friends and strangers,

eagerly clutching the last breath of my question and the first breath of their reply. And in between obsessing over whether or not he would call, I regularly checked voice mail to see if he did. I was banking on his mercy, but perhaps I was too generous with my expectation of compassion, seeing as how he was dogging me every step of the way. Anticipation deposited me in the vicinity of madness. Would he have a change of heart and call? Would he care enough to drip an ounce of water on my inextinguishable yearning for the sound of his voice? God, I hoped so.

I felt sluggish as I sat on the edge of my bed and literally tried to restrain my heart from exiting through the other side of my skin. I wanted to cry again, but I was too stubborn to give way to grand emotion behind another loser. Another king without a queen because he had chosen to play the field instead of settling down and making babies. Another guy that I would eventually talk myself into allowing between my legs because I promised myself that this one was different and this time was special.

And, in the end, who winds up with crushed bones and a broken spirit? The idealistic, oversimplified, unrealistic dreamer whose animated expression does well to be placed under this appropriate category: S-U-C-K-E-R.

It was time for a heart-to-heart with Jesus, so I concluded the evening down on my knees.

Dear Jesus,

Again, I am weeping the departure of another one of your beautiful creatures.

What am I doing wrong? Is it every other guy in the world or is it just me? Certainly I delight in the intellectual man, but perhaps I am much too drawn to physical aspects.

Is it the way their arms ripple with muscle? The way their chest rises and falls with their breath or perhaps the way their brows rise with seduction? I am carnal and basic in my search for a mate, giving too much regard to exterior walls, shallow water, and hollow ground.

I was always taught in the temple of worship to seek out a man who loves the Lord, but Jesus . . . they're all geeks. No offense, but they lack polish and pizzazz, and once a girl has been with the Cadillac of the male species, a Plymouth Duster will no longer do. Once a girl experiences the most beautiful that a breed has to offer, wrapping bare knuckles around a rock-hard butt or playing tic-tac-toe on a six-pack, it's hard, if not damn near impossible, to switch to ordinary. Sorry Jesus, I didn't mean to be so explicit.

The nice guys like me, but I don't like the nice guys back. It's never even. He will want me more than I can stand to be wanted or I will want him more than he deserves or can accept. If this is the way it's supposed to unfold and solo is my destiny, then Jesus please be courteous enough to provide me with two essentials: one pair of extraordinary eyes capable of finding beauty in solitude and a ready-made heart eager to accept the status of being alone.

Amen.

I crawled into bed with new resolution and a desire to change. I would no longer worship a man because he was beautiful. I would be selective and focus more on the spirit that moves him than the tight, muscular legs and penis length. I nearly floated to sleep on that last thought, but notice I said, "nearly."

My doorbell rang at 11:57 P.M.

I squinted, looking at the clock again for clarification: 11:58 P.M.

"What the hell?" I asked, pulling a tired back and heavy heart from the comfort of my queen-size mattress. I always slept in the nude, so I had to scramble to find a robe to cover chilled brown skin. When I finally got myself together, I shuffled to the door and glanced through the peephole to see what jerk would possibly entertain his presence in my world at such an inappropriate hour.

"Oh, my God," I mouthed the words in silence. "Oh, my God," I said again, fidgeting at the doorway, shifting my weight from one foot to the other. My palms began to sweat, and I laid one hand on my chest in what would prove to be a futile attempt to stabilize an erratic heartbeat.

I swung the door open, trying not to look desperate.

"Eddie?"

He looked down for a moment.

"I forgot something," he said.

"What?" I replied quickly, barely letting him get the words out.

"I forgot to teach you how to ride a bike."

I looked away, not sure what to think or how to feel.

"It's really late," I noted.

"I know," he said gently. "Sorry."

"I miss you so much," I blurted out, and it came from nowhere.

I pulled the door open wide and took one step backward, leaving a gap between us. The opening was his invite and he accepted. Once he was inside, I shut the door.

There was only one dim light burning in my apartment, and he walked to that light and turned it off. As he walked, I clocked every move, translating each step into poetry. Tears began forming in my eyes. "Eddie," I called his name out loud.

He approached me slowly.

As he stood before me, I reflected on every reason why I should tell him to get out of my house and never return. He had abandoned me and slept with another woman, the worst of relationship sins.

He had demolished my self-esteem and trampled on my dreams. How could I allow him to stand here, remove my clothing, and slide his hands over my sacred parts? Forbidden places? And Magic Kingdom? The answer was as simple as the question. Every single aspect of his being, from the way he walked, to the way he talked, to the way his eyebrows arched in the middle, to the dent of every muscle under his skin, to his scent, taste, touch, skin, and even drops of semen, I craved them all.

"You're no good for me, Eddie," I whispered fondling his erection. His clothing slipped to the floor and there he stood, naked in the arch of my doorway like artwork without an artist to claim him.

"Beautiful," I said staring. "Beautiful, beautiful, beautiful," I said again and again as I dropped to my knees and satisfied his basic instinct.

"Ooooooohhhhh," he moaned squeezing my head between his hands.

I laid myself down and pulled him close, pulled him so close that it would be impossible for him not to penetrate me. On my floor, I satisfied and was satisfied till I was raw and my uterus posted a sign declaring "No Entry." My skin was numb and my back was scratched and chaffed. His face was flushed and both of us panted like dogs, the aftermath of too much deep breathing and too little water. After we had stopped moving there was nothing left to say except, "Good night."

"Good night?" I said franticly, shocked that he was dressing to leave. "Eddie," I said, sounding desperate but not meaning to. "Why can't you just stay till morning?"

He smiled as he pulled his shirt over a majestically carved chest. My eyes scanned the length of him. *Dear Jesus, I want this man so bad that I taste him in my sleep.* "It's already morning," he said, shooting me down.

"Then stay and let me hold you till the sun comes up," I begged.

I know I looked pathetic, but I couldn't help myself. I was so scared to let him walk out the door because it would be weeks, to months, to forever that I would ever hear from him again. Every time we parted the gap grew longer before we would meet again. And in between those meetings, I would blister, literally blister.

"The sun isn't coming up today. It's supposed to rain, remember?" he asked, gently kissing me on the forehead. "I'll call you later," he said briskly moving toward an exit.

"Why can't you be honest with me?" I asked in a voice trembling with emotion.

He sighed and stopped walking, but refused to turn around and face me.

"Why can't you just be for real, Eddie?"

And finally, he did turn around. "What do you want me to say?"

"What is it with you? Why did you come here?" I asked.

"I don't know," he said, head hung low.

I threw up my hands and shouted, "You can't keep doing this to me! Taking me on this roller coaster ride!"

Agitated, he shook his head, "Boy, you really know how to ruin a perfectly good evening."

When I saw the look on his face and heard the harshness of his words—I snapped.

"Correction. It wasn't an evening—an evening begins just before sundown. So don't flatter yourself. It was a midnight booty call and there's nothing perfect about that, so get over yourself!"

"What do you want from me?" he said, piercing me with a disturbed gaze. "What? What are you looking for, Michael?"

"I want you to stay," I said going out on a limb. "I want you to want the same things that I do. I'm so tired of the push and pull with you and me, Eddie. Come and go and go and go and leave . . ." By the time I was able to spit out the last word, I was nearly hysterical.

Eddie stood in the doorway expressionless. The story could have tilted either direction. He could have broken down and embraced me, accepted my love as it was, pure or impure as it seemed to be, or he could have opened the door and walked out. The moment was tense and intense. And the only bonding glue to the situation were tears, my tears.

"I can't give you that," he said. "I don't want the same things you do. I don't feel the same way you do . . ."

"Why?" I asked, pleading for understanding. "Why can't you feel this magic between us?"

He looked at me as though I were an idiot. As though I were a mental patient on a weekend pass from the nuthouse. "This isn't what magic feels like to me," he said bluntly.

"Then why did you come here tonight?" I asked point black with a straight face and no emotion.

"I wanted to see you," he said.

"Why did you come here tonight?" I pressed.

"I said—"

"Bullshit," I said sharply.

He almost laughed, a nervous laugh though. "What do you want to hear, Michael?"

"Something you're probably incapable of . . . the truth."

"I wanted to see you," he said. "Why are you making this into more than it is?"

"You son-of-a-bitch! I'm standing here bleeding all over

myself! You think you can just drop in and out of my life like a freaking yo-yo . . . that you can take me on a roller coaster ride, up and down, and down and down for kicks. You think you can just walk in here . . ."

"I don't need this shit," he said walking away. When he turned his back on me, I became infuriated and scared. I wanted to build a cage around him and prevent his departure. To hell with the "If you love something set it free theory . . ." I wanted to gift wrap him in chains because I couldn't bear the thought of living my life without him. I felt insane, but I just couldn't help myself. There was something about the energy that danced around this man that I wanted to own.

"Why didn't you just call the blonde and leave me the hell alone!" I screamed.

He stopped, turned around, and said, "I did call her but she wasn't home."

I don't remember much after that, except for the violence. I remember the commotion of an assault on Eddie that early morning. I raged out of control and bum rushed him. I slightly remember pounding my fist into his chest, yelling obscenities, demanding compensation for my pain, releasing anger and wrath without thought of a consequence. I don't remember much else, except of course crying myself to sleep that morning in my doorway, rocking dead air in my arms for comfort. Somehow Eddie had managed to slip from my clutches that night, from my arms and my life for good.

So again, in the end who gets hurt? For the record let it be duly noted that the idealistic, oversimplified, unrealistic dreamer whose animated expression does well to be placed under the only category able to sustain it: S-U-C-K-E-R.

23

REAL MEN DON'T BEND HEARTS

The days following my attack on Eddie were cruel.

A week had given birth to a month, to six weeks and counting since our altercation.

Molly was still standing behind her "stale pussy" theory and Sky was convinced that the only way beyond the pain was through it. So I took off my shoes and began the long, painful road to recovery. Beyond the devastation of the breakup, I was mortified at my erratic and unpredictable behavior, resorting to shouting, kicking, screaming, and hitting. It was so untypical of me, so unbecoming to a lady and a sane person. Had I become my mother by accident when I wasn't looking?

I went on with my life, so to speak, easing back into my daily routine. I had missed so many days from work that fixing up the dead was my full-time job and kissing Mr. Tucker's ass had become my part-time one. But Eddie was never far from my mind and, unfortunately, still the topic of many of my conversations, like this one at breakfast with Sky.

"I can't believe you're still sulking over this guy," said Sky without regard for my fragility. "You only dated him a few months, baby. It's not like he was the last man. Your grief is lasting longer than the relationship."

"Well, thank you for your compassion," I said sarcastically. "And understanding and sensitivity—"

"Michael, I'm sorry," he said, rubbing my arm, trying to sooth the raw. "I just don't like seeing you like this."

"Then maybe you shouldn't see me," I said, before taking a gulp of coffee that was too hot. "Damn," I said, rubbing burned lips.

Sky quieted and so did I.

The silence wrestled between us for a while.

"What do you miss about him?" he asked. "What do you really miss?"

"He's the only man that I've ever been with that didn't make me feel like he was just *fucking* me," I said. And boy, you should have seen the look on Sky's face after that statement.

Ouch.

"And his smile," I said, staring out the window. "His eyes. Dimples. Laugh. His touch. And spirit."

"His disappearance, disloyalty, and cheating," Sky said sharply. "And don't forget to add midnight booty calls to your list."

My eyes narrowed.

"I'm just trying to get you to be real, baby," he said reaching for me, but I pushed back from the table. "If you're going to walk on the dream you need to stand on the reality," he said.

"You were his flavor of the month, Michael. Don't you get it? It's a new month now."

My scrambled eggs dried up and almost slithered off the table. My coffee went down the wrong pipe forcing me to gag and spit. It appeared that no one in the restaurant moved, or breathed, or judged, except me.

I had been officially declared *Boo Boo the Fool*. Maybe he was using me for sex. Maybe they all used me for sex, and no one ever cared. Maybe the best I could get was a mercy lay from Sky, who for all intents and purposes seemed about as asexual as a man could be.

For there are certain truths that need not be told when they only serve to crush the one to whom they are directed. Sky felt the need to say it, but he didn't have to because I already knew it. And even if I didn't truly know it, I didn't feel it was his place to tell me at all.

I laid twenty dollars on the table, enough for my breakfast and his, got up, and walked out, leaving Sky alone. I needed to be by myself so I could sort things out.

But where do I go from here?

Antonio's back bent into a deep arch.

I panted.

And moaned.

I dug my nails into his flesh because it felt so good to be so bad.

251

"I missed you," I panted, barely able to find my breath, much less catch it. "Missed you so much."

He yelled something in Spanish, which I didn't understand, but from what I was able to decipher, his orgasm was on the way. I hadn't seen Antonio in months because I had given up casual sex in exchange for a more destructive vice, falling in love with the wrong guy, *again*.

Once we finished pounding each other's flesh, it was done and there was nothing else to say, at least not on my part. What else was there to talk about that he could actually understand? Antonio was primarily Spanish-speaking, remember?

"Practicar," he said, kneeling in front of me.

I sat on the bed, dumbfounded and naked. "Huh?"

"Practicar. Practice *mi* English?"

I smiled, gently rubbing his face. "You want to practice your English. How sweet. When?"

He lit up with enthusiasm. *"Ahora."*

I took that to mean *now*.

"Okay," I said, bunching up a sheet, modestly covering my nakedness. "I am ready to be your tutor."

"¿Por què?" he asked with eyes lowering to sadness.

"Antonio, what's wrong?" I asked, rubbing his shoulders with concern and empathy.

"Why so sad?" he asked, staring deeply into my eyes.

I started laughing, trying to shake off the blatant truth. "I'm not sad, baby . . ."

"Tu corazón," he said pointing to my chest. *"Es* broken."

In any language, in every language, a broken heart is a broken heart. I looked away because I did not have the courage to face him. God, am I so pathetic that this boy can see my pain? Can he read the hurt of my heart like braille? Can he see through my bullshit just by opening his eyes?

"Not broken," I assured. "Just a little bent," I said, demonstrating with hand gestures the words I was trying to convey.

"Who bent you?" he asked.

I laughed out loud. His English had improved considerably since the last time we met, but it was still a competitive distance away from good.

"A boy," I replied.

"*Un niño o un hombre?*" he asked.

I was confused by his native tongue so he broke it down in English for me. "A boy or a man?" he asked.

I smiled shyly as the following word echoed from my voice box, "Man."

"No, if he bent you, he was no man. Real men don't bend hearts . . . beautiful heart."

"Wow," I said softening. "You learned a new word, *beautiful*. Who taught you beautiful?"

He began stroking the side of my face with deliberate tenderness. And without grand warning, I grabbed him and held on till his warmth became my warmth. And my warmth became his. Now this truly was original, a repeat one-night stand floats its way to the surface to step out of the box and take a peek at the real thing, for a minute. But only for a minute.

———

"You've gone mad," I hissed, leaning over the corpse of an obese forty-seven-year-old woman who had dropped dead of a heart attack. But it wasn't really the corpse I was talking to lest I be the one you think had gone mad. It was my intellectually deprived coworker, Timm. He was staging a reenactment of his scandalous weekend, passing around gossip like an old catty bitch.

"So, I saw your old boyfriend Saturday night," he said.

"Eddie?" I asked, perking up.

"Yeah . . . that's the hot white guy you were seeing, right? The one that came up here . . ."

"Yeah, yeah, yeah . . ." I said, pushing past the details.

"I thought so," he said like a sly fox.

"Oh, here we go," I said, gripping the side of the table. "So, who was he with? I know you can't wait to tell me."

"He was by himself," he said with a stupid grin.

"And?" I said, struggling to restrain my "I can't stand you" declaration till after he had told me everything I wanted to know.

"He looked good," he said nodding, procrastinating. "He was going into Blue Jay's," he said smiling.

"That's it?" I asked. "So what's the big deal?"

"He was going into Blue Jay's," he repeated slower, pulling on the words, stretching them out for me to absorb. "Blue Jay's."

"So what?"

"He was in the market for a hooker," he said casually.

"No, he wasn't!"

"He sure wasn't going there for the food."

"How do you know?" I asked.

"They don't serve food at Blue Jay's," he said about to pop at the seams. "They serve *hookers*."

"Whatever," I replied flippantly, but my heart felt like it was being squeezed.

"So you're over this guy, huh?"

"Totally," I said without flinching.

"Wow, I'm really impressed at the way you've moved beyond this."

"You oughta be," I said with a little cocky in my attitude.

"Girlfriend, teach me a thing or two about getting over a broken heart."

"And you know I can," I boasted.

"Girl, I would just flip if someone I cared about was on the prowl for streetwalkers and paid blow jobs."

Timm was pulling my chain, trying to let the mad dog lose. Damn him for stressing me like this.

"Well, that's just it, I don't care about him anymore."

"Not at all?"

"Not a beat," I confirmed.

The next morning I called off work.

Again.

24

THE UNTURNED CARD

Sometimes today shows up juggling yesterday in one hand, tomorrow in the other. That's when you know you have no chance of winning at all. And that was quickly becoming my reality.

Tucker laid me off from the funeral home, a devastating blow I was too numb to feel. He cited the "business slowing down" as the reason for my dismissal. Yeah, right. His fictitious explanation didn't slide down easily because people die every day and dead people will always be around. But I didn't argue with his decision to let me go. After all, I had been missing beats for some time now. I had exhausted my sick leave, drained my vacation days, and clocked countless hours of unaccounted time for mental health issues.

Last week I really blew it when a nineteen-year-old girl had to be laid to rest in an old-lady wig because I didn't show up to do her hair.

And again I had nothing to offer but silence as Tucker screamed at me behind closed doors. When he demanded an explanation, I had none to give because sometimes the truth is just flat-out unacceptable. It is then that we are forced to become storytellers and illusion artists creating pictures that don't exist and worlds that aren't real. What could I say? *I'm sorry that this child who died before her time was put to rest in an old woman's wig because it hurts me too bad to get out of bed in the morning. I let you down because I am constant agony over a simple thing, a man. I can't show up for work on time because I lay in my bed and cry all night till exhaustion rocks me to sleep. And then it keeps me there way past my wake-up call. I can't hold a consistent thought because this guy's face, essence, presence, scent, and touch are attached to every neurotransmitter in my head.* Is this really what you want to hear? If I spoke the absolute blatant truth as to why I didn't show up and do her hair, you would surely leap across your desk, place your bare hands around my neck, and strangle what you would perceive at this point, a life not worth living. So in answer to your question of what went wrong? "I apologize sir. I overslept."

The pink slip was in my box by day's end.

I returned to what felt like the only safe place I still had left, Sky's house.

I knocked on his door and he answered.

He didn't look happy to see me nor did he look sad. He didn't look as if he were ready to embrace me nor shoo me away. He didn't look fond of me nor did he appear to dislike me. He held steady at neutral, but sometimes neutral is the most difficult position of all because it refuses to bend one way or the other.

"Hello," I finally said because somebody had to break.

"Hello," he replied without grand emotion.

"Do you hate me?" I asked under the assumption that the answer was yes. Why wouldn't he hate me? Of course he did. Look at what a loser I had turned out to be.

"No, I don't hate you Michael," he said calmly. "I just find you unbearably draining these days."

"Oh," I said lowering my head.

"But I don't hate you," he said.

"Thanks for clarifying that," I said somewhat sarcastically. And to my surprise, he smiled.

And I smiled.

And soon, he laughed out loud.

And soon, so did I.

And then he stopped and so did I, both unsure of where to go from here. I was convinced that Sky was over our relationship, so done and outdone. So tired and distant, removed but still there. Relationships like ours weren't the norm. We had made love, destroyed love, and still found a common ground to meet in the middle on friendship. Sky always had me guessing on the nature of his unturned card and why we couldn't be together.

"Am I welcome here?" I asked.

He opened the door wide so I could enter. There was something about his presence that had always made the hair stand up on the back of my neck. There was something venomously intoxicating about him, which drew me to be by his side.

He sat down on the couch and patted the seat beside him, gesturing that I join him. And without much coercion at all, I jumped at the chance to be close.

He picked up the remote and began changing channels and for a moment it felt like old times again. But old times brought back old, nagging thoughts.

Show me your cards, I wanted to shout. *Show me your unturned cards.*

The chemistry began sucking on my skin and opening my pores. It was powerful, and it called me to him. I could feel his arousal in my presence, and I could also feel mine. But with our last intimate tragedy firmly embedded in mind and body, I was not so quick to respond until it became unbearable. And only then did I reach for him and stroke his chest, slowly.

He grabbed my hand, stopping me midstroke.

He looked at me and I at him and we both gave way to uncomfortable. But I didn't want to stop the seduction because I needed to know that someone found me attractive and appealing, enticing and alluring.

I moved closer to him, softly kissing his cheek. He shut his eyes and began drifting. I kissed him again and again. He didn't stop me, nor did he encourage me to continue.

My lips moved from his cheek, to his chin, then to his stomach. My tongue followed with ease his abdominal muscles as they protruded through his skin, down to the fly of his jeans.

And then I stopped, looked up, and waited for permission to continue.

What was I doing? Was I stepping on hot coals once again because I derived sick pleasure from the sensation of burning flesh? There was a pause in the flow. I didn't know if I should continue or retard the journey and return to the safe end of the sofa. We could flip through the channels and search for a Johnny Carson classic to kill the awkwardness of the moment. *Give me some direction here,* I wanted to ask. This was really confusing. Do you want me to do this thing or not? Are you able to receive my affection with the same intensity that I am delivering it to you? Or is this whole thing a stretch, a struggle?

I opened my mouth and inserted him inside. And he moaned just as I knew he would. I stayed there while Sky did what men naturally do when their privates are swallowed by the suction of lips, teeth, and tongue. Milky white leaked down my chin and I wiped it away with my fingers.

He gently moved me aside so that he could go to the bathroom and rinse me away. I walked into his kitchen and gargled my mouth with saltwater. When I returned to the couch he was sitting on the opposite end, lifeless.

I picked up the remote and clicked on a channel, any channel. The first station I hit was airing a Johnny Carson classic.

Imagine that.

25

ON MY KNEES

Time moved, but I stayed and the days progressed without me. I was living off my savings, credit cards, and borrowed time. I was sleeping till noon and drinking till midnight. And in between those hours I was trying to convince everyone, including myself, that I was okay.

I had begun a new relationship, one that I was getting pretty serious about. It was a sweet but debilitating affair with chocolate ice cream and candy-coated sprinkles. It was a love-hate relationship between my mouth and my hips.

I was shopping for new outfits on a daily basis, but I wasn't interested in clothes, at least not ordinary ones. I was searching for magic fabric, the kind that would make me more lovable. The kind that would make him and him and him long for me.

I needed the right kind of cloth, the one that would make me irresistible. I needed the right color, texture, style, and fit to take away the lonely. And even though I was unemployed, cost was no option. Actually, cost was every option, but I couldn't hang a price tag on my self-esteem. The more desperate I became, the tighter the dress, the shorter the skirt, the lower the blouse. Tragic, isn't it?

I was pulling in more men than I could keep track of. There were tall ones, short ones, rich ones, poor ones. There were convicts and conflicts. There were Mercedes drivers and bus riders. There were hustlers and busters. There were mama's boys, sugar daddies, and absentee fathers. There were fine ones and finer ones. There were gym goers and paper pushers. They were businessmen and bullshitters. And they all had my number. I had a date every night of the week, capturing the title "Professional Girlfriend in Training."

Monday night.

Grayson.

Six foot four. Creole descent. Fair skin. Green eyes. Body of a god. Face of a centerfold. We captured the evening lakeside from a restaurant that hung from a cliff. The sun was low, the moon high. I bought whatever it was he was selling. He was everything from the star quarterback of his college football team to the first-round draft pick for NFL. He was the neighborhood Casanova and the state of Colorado's Don Juan Demarco.

He was fly.

Hip.

Ambitious.

Bright.

Articulate.

And pretty as the day is long.

Men wanted to be him and women just wanted to be *with* him.

The night was perfect. I couldn't have knocked on Jesus' door and asked for better weather or better food, a more pleasant atmosphere, a more awesome view, a more beautiful dress, or a more elegant man to complement my high-dollar look. But in all that was good or better, I found myself ordering one glass of wine after the other to sooth the beast of l-o-n-e-l-y.

Grayson's external shell was off the hook and that much was inarguable. He was by far the most beautiful breathing mammal in the restaurant, and that, too, was inarguable. But if it were up to me, I would draw up a disclaimer and stick it to the back of his ass:

Dear Consumer, This man is fine as hell, but he is also self-centered, self-consumed, self-absorbed, and self-appointed as The Last Man Standing on Earth.

He is preoccupied with his own achievements, unevolved, and in love with being in love with himself. Every eloquent word that spills from his gorgeous mouth will only emphasize an overinflated ego and underdeveloped sense of what's really going on.

He is the man every woman dreams of, but after a long night without anesthesia (i.e., beer, wine, wine cooler, straight vodka, or the crack pipe), you will find yourself fleeing the scene, falling from a cloud, all the while vehemently searching for the street sign with a giant green arrow that reads: "Back to Earth . . . this way."

Good night, Grayson.

Damn.

Tuesday, Wednesday, and Thursday offered no redemption.

On Tuesday, there was aspiring singer Damon James. He was broke, desperate, and much like the others, caught up in the hype that he was really something special (*catching the number-two bus and transferring to the thirteen is not a job skill, so please get over yourself*).

Damon claimed he was in the studio recording an album for a record company based in Tempe, Arizona. We had made plans for dinner and I made the mistake of allowing him to choose the restaurant. Since his alleged automobile was in the shop (read between the lines: I *am* a year-round bus rider), out of pity, I volunteered to pick him up. But I should have snatched back my invite for a ride when the bootlegger couldn't provide an *exact* address. "Make a left here and then a right and pull into the alley and flash your lights and I'll appear . . ." *What the blankety, blank, blank was that all about?* And how stupid did I look following those directions? "Right . . . Left . . . okay . . . here's the alley . . . let me flash my lights . . ." When he got in the car I eased up a bit because he looked so good. I couldn't believe that such a fine man could be on foot.

"Hey, pretty girl," he said, offering a kiss on the cheek.

"Hey," I said. He proceeded to direct me to a diner in the middle of a hoodlum-infested, gang-controlled neighborhood. "Great, I'm wearing red," I said sarcastically as I pulled my car into the parking lot.

"Oh, baby," he said. "It ain't that deep."

"Then why did you request a table away from the window?" I asked him after we had sat down.

"Because my bulletproof vest is in the cleaners," he said with a stupid grin on his face.

"Get what you want, baby," he said as we glanced through the menu.

"Thank you," I responded before I heard him say. "May as well . . . you're paying for it."

Good night, Damon.

On Wednesday I went out with Lloyd, a parole officer by day, psychic by night. By the end of the date, I'm sure Lloyd didn't need to consult his crystal ball to figure out I was never seeing his weird ass again.

Thursday I went out with Duncan, a professional disc jockey. Okay. This one was a real shocker. Duncan was attractive, kind, and normal. He didn't spend the evening victimized by hallucinations of a life well lived. He was humble, a trait that I was starting to believe was only found in pigs before they were slaughtered for their bacon. He didn't ramble on about his conquests and accomplishments. He didn't stand up, beat his chest, and exact testosterone from his mighty fangs. He wasn't overly aggressive or unduly passive. He didn't push, bend, or rub me the wrong way. I was convinced of his sexual orientation, a real bonus. He owned transportation and, unlike Damon, had enough cash to pay not only for the bill but also for the tip. And this led me to believe that I could be with him, not forever of course, because I was still feeling Eddie, but I could bank on one night. So, after dinner we went back to my place where heavy petting set the stage for the next disaster in my life.

He was doing all the right things in all the right places. His lips were soft, smooth. He could speak three languages—English, Portuguese, and Spanish—and he called out my name in all three.

"Oh, baby," I moaned thinking I could really go there. I could give him one authentic moment.

This might happen.

This could happen.

This will happen.

"Oh, my God . . . this can't happen!" I jumped from the bed, screaming. He looked mortified because he knew I had seen it.

"Oh, my God," I said running to the bathroom where I slammed the door. "Why didn't you tell me?" I shouted. "Why?!"

He didn't answer.

I sat on the toilet and put my head between my legs trying not to throw up. He didn't answer. After several minutes I heard the echo of footsteps, the closing of the front door, complete silence, and then I knew he was gone.

I didn't want to be cruel but I just couldn't believe it. When he removed his clothing in the dark and I went to stroke his skin with my hands, I wound up fondling his colon-replacement bag instead.

On Friday I was too traumatized to go on another date.

Seventy-two chicken wings in a bucket with a flap that leaked grease around the edges, that was my peace offering to the eccentric mystic. I rang her bell once, twice, then knocked rhythmically on the splintered door because I needed her fat ass to open up for business. Desperation didn't come packaged any tighter than that.

"Mabel!" I shouted into a creepy nearby window trying to peek inside.

I know your fat ass is in there, Mabel. I can hear you breathing.

My life was unraveling like a giant spool of thread while this fickle fortune-teller chose to give into her temperamental nature.

Come on Mabel, dammit.

I raised myself on the tip of my toes and leaned into the kitchen window with two hands cupped around my eyes for easy viewing.

Two ugly red eyes stared back. Immediately, I backed up.

Damn. What kind of voodoo does the woman do today?

"Hi, Mabel," I smiled, raising the chicken wings up high, hoping they would intercept the lead bullet if she started tripping. "Can we talk?" I asked with more humility than usual.

She didn't respond.

"Mabel," I called again. "Can I talk to you?"

Her eyes bled from red to redder as she held an affectation of silence.

"I need your help, Mabel," I said. "Please?" I asked nicely. "Please?"

She closed the curtain tightly and I caught a glimpse of her shadow as it exited the kitchen. I thought the old broad was coming to let me in. Of course I would have to endure a brisk frisk and a hellified shakedown, but still she'd let me in, or so I thought. But to my surprise, Mabel didn't open the door that day. I was parked on her doorstep for seventeen minutes and the heifer didn't let me in.

I placed my ear against the door and there were no signs of life. I couldn't even hear breathing so I sat the chicken wings down on the step and left.

Damn Mabel, you sure picked a fine day to start acting up.

Molly was one day from release and we were sitting in our usual spot, contemplating the usual things.

"One day to freedom," I reminded her. "Are you ready?"

"Yeah, I'm ready to blow this Popsicle stand," she said less confident than usual.

"What are you going to do when you get out?" I asked her.

"Get wasted," she said only half kidding. "No, I'm cool honey bunny," she confirmed, trying to clean it up for my benefit.

"You going back to work?" I asked cautiously.

"There will always be a John in need of a Molly," she said sarcastically. And that was her way of telling me yes without disappointing me with the truth. Yet, we would not contemplate her stuff for long because we would quickly hop onto mine and the tone would change. "So what are you going to do about your nose?" She asked with a nervy judgmental eye.

"Nothing," I responded flatly.

"I see you've come to your senses," she declared.

"No, I've come to realize that without a job it just won't happen," I snapped.

I could feel a wall rise between us. But I could shut her down just like that or snap our friendship in half like a wishbone. If she pushed too hard today, the camel's back would break and we would cease communication till somebody got lonely and desperate. My PMS was bigger than her PMS, even if she was going through heroin withdrawals.

"You still messing with that fucking guy?" she asked.

I didn't answer and that told her everything she needed to know.

"Michael, you've got to leave him alone," she said puffing a Virginia Slim. "Didn't you ever see that movie, *Fatal Attraction?*"

Ouch.

"I'll leave him alone as soon you leave them alone," I said pointing to her cigarettes. She took a deep breath, threw down the cigarette, and stepped on it for confirmation.

"You'll be back for it," I said staring at the butt as it stuck through the ground.

"And so will you," she said. "Bet?"

"Oh, girl," I said blowing her off. "You'd lose."

"Then bet me," she said extending a hand.

"I don't want to take your money like that," I said.

"Why not? I'd take yours."

"Okay, tough girl. How long can you go without a cigarette?" I asked glancing at my watch.

"About an hour," she snapped quickly.

"Then you'd lose," I confirmed.

"Don't think so," she spouted with confidence.

"Excuse me 'Proud Mary,' but sixty minutes without a ciga-rette is not a staggering amount of time."

"Maybe . . . but it's still ten minutes *longer* than you can go without that guy," she said, driving home the punch line with a smile. Certain jest eased its way into something that wasn't so funny. There was a handful of truth in what had just been said. There was something funny about it and nothing humorous about it at all. My situation with Eddie transcended human degradation. I knew that, and until I could get beyond it, I would never feel good about myself.

"Can't you just walk away?" she asked looking at me like *I* was the one in rehab. Shit, maybe I should have been in rehab. "We're not talking about a heroin addiction here. He's just a guy. I can fuck a different guy every day and not get attached," she said as though boasting of some special God-given gift.

"But you're a prostitute, Molly," I said, stating the obvious and hoping not to offend her, but insistent upon making a point. "You can't afford attachment."

"Funny thing is," she said reaching for another cigarette, "neither can you."

"Looks like all bets are off," I declared as I watched her light up without apology. She didn't acknowledge the cigarette nor the wager we almost made. And that was so typical of Molly, liv-ing life in a way that would always spell *convenient* for her.

"I feel like I'm going to die without him," I said. "That probably doesn't make sense to you . . ."

"HELLO!" she yelled. "I am a drug addict! *Everything* makes sense to me. But the question is, does it make sense to you?"

26

SAVVY GRAVY

None of it made sense to me.

I allowed one month to pass and still yet another.

No sense.

No sense.

No sense it made to me.

Molly Wood was out of rehab and probably back on the block again, but we never talked about it. It wasn't polite to bring it up, so we managed to find ways to talk around it.

"How's work?" I asked.

"Steady," she'd say with a period on the end of that sentence.

My mother finally retired from her day job as the church secretary, just in the nick of time to start getting old. Our relationship settled into polite interaction.

Nothing deep.

Nothing profound.

Just polite.

Mr. Tucker hired another dream weaver and dead bodies continued to show up at his door. My ex coworker, Timm, and

I eventually stopped speaking and we downgraded our relation-ship from friend to acquaintance.

Sky and I settled in as "just friends" because he had finally come out of the closet and revealed that he was gay. He con-fessed to having known it for some time now, but also said he lacked the courage to accept it.

Sky moved to another state to start a new life and disconnect from the old one. He promised to keep in touch but didn't keep his word.

And the beat goes on.

And on and on.

And the sun still rises, sets, and returns again. And in the midst of all life happening, I still could not manage to shake my frantic infatuation with a man that I still could not seem to breathe easy without.

What had happened to my great love affair with the man I loved so much? Should I grieve our unborn children knowing they shall never take up residency outside the fantasy world I created in my head? And what about the dress I would have worn to our wedding? And the vows I would have said, given the grand opportunity? When I peeled away the dream I could see my vows, one letter at a time, roll off the edge of my tongue and splatter to the ground before they could be heard or consummated.

Damn you Eddie for throwing us in the trash. We could have been contenders for the future. Isn't that worth fighting for? I convinced myself that it was. Perhaps that was the only way to justify another unannounced visit to his home, early one evening after leaving my mother's home.

How will your face twist with disappointment this time? I thought as I turned onto his street. *How will you hold your stance and impair your posture while struggling to deal with me on your doorstep again?*

If you ask if I am desperate, I shall reply, "I am."

Will you devour me like fresh salmon and deliver me unseasoned on the platter of my chagrin? Are you here again? I almost hear him ask. Are you here again? The faint echo of unspoken words sashays around the ordinary, meticulous plotting of my emotional demise. Are you here again? I ask, are you here again?

"Will he hate me for this?" I asked myself straddling sanity. Will he hate me for showing up on his doorstep again, without an invitation in the middle of the night? He had been very specific about us being "done."

Stick a fork in it lady, we're done.

"Okay," I mumbled, pretending that I would actually honor those words. But I never listened. And time and time again I popped over, unannounced, setting myself up for devastation, hurt feelings and a life that was about to change forever.

He didn't answer, but I didn't expect him to because I barely knocked. An illusionist couldn't have called it closer: *now did the girl knock or didn't she?* I was playing the "chicken role." If I knocked too hard, he might actually *open* the door. And how could I insist upon that? I couldn't. And that's the reason I didn't knock, I think. At best, it was an exhausting mind game, trying to salvage a dignity that I was not the rightful owner of in the first place. I didn't have the heart to stomach rejection so I stood on his doorstep like the Avon lady, believing in the eventuality of our paths crossing again. Parking yourself on somebody's front yard is an optimal way of ensuring a second meeting, I believed.

I coughed. It wasn't your everyday kind of cough. It was more of a nervous cough. An "Oh, my God, I must look like a retard on your front step" kind of cough. Or better yet, an "If you open the door I will fall easy prey to urinary-incontinence-kind-of-cough." Yeah, it was that kind of cough for sure.

I calculated a dismal future under overcast skies that had lightly started to break with rain. The first few drops landing on my scalp sent me into hysteria. Do you know what rain does to a press-and-curl? Ethnicity was a beautiful thing, but an afro contradicted my denim outfit, so I abandoned the doorstep in search of full-bodied shelter on his backyard patio.

Damn, Eddie, can you say "*lawn man?*" The backyard looked like an on-location shoot for National Geographic. The only thing missing were people running around in grass skirts and nose rings made of animal bone. High grass and higher weeds added to the distasteful Amazon decor. I wrestled shrubbery and bushes to save my wilting hairdo and make it to the patio, which I finally did.

As I tilted into position, I saw that the patio door was

unlocked, which meant anyone who slid it open was granted automatic access into his world.

I was frightened by the thought and didn't do anything for about three minutes because I wanted to take time and think about the repercussions of breaking and entering. Actually, I wasn't breaking anything, so I wouldn't be charged with breaking, but I could be slammed with an "entering without an invitation" charge. But that didn't sound like the worst thing to be convicted of. He could press charges, but I doubt he would. Didn't I have privilege to his world by virtue of the fact that I had swallowed his sperm once, maybe even twice? That noble gesture alone granted me unrestricted access, right?

End of discussion—or maybe not. If he adopted the unpopular theory that I was a nuisance, he could appeal for public sympathy, and if he went as far as attaching *stalker* to the label, he could justifiably issue a restraining order against me. *But how malicious would that be?*

In all fairness, if I put myself in his shoes, I could understand the pungent taste I had left in his mouth. I had shown up consistently on his door against his wishes and repeatedly disrespected his privacy. I had backed his masculinity and sexuality into a corner and forced him to respond to my oral seduction. I had watched his attempt to tolerate my invasions and deal with them poetically and I hadn't cared at all about the struggle. But what about my struggle, my pain and punitive damages as I rapidly succumbed to such an embarrassing display?

I didn't take pride in home invasion, but I couldn't help myself. It was a desperation-driven, man-made obsession for that *thing* I could not have. It was the dream that I still believed existed, but to actually reach it, touch it, grab it, and hold on left me in the company of empty air.

It was a deep cry on a dark night for a light that wouldn't shine or a chill that could not be warmed by the flame. I didn't wake up today with eager anticipation of being a stalker, and if a stalker was what I had become it was purely accidental in its progression. It was likened to the splash of pee that leaks out between a laugh or the involuntary release of gas that refused to stay confined to the inside. At best, it was embarrassing, humiliating, and somewhat degrading, but in the end it was all so *necessary*.

I hadn't seen Eddie's Jeep out front so I was certain he wasn't home. I put my hand against the door and pushed a little, but it opened a lot.

Nervous energy, it blows holes through doors every time.

I felt cool escape. The circular fans were calling me inside to dodge humidity. *What to do? What to do?*

If I step through this convenient gap in the door, which is just large enough to fit my breasts and butt through, I'll add a new job skill to my budding résumé: *criminal.* But if I close the door right now and go home, maybe, just maybe in about six or seven years, I'll be able to forgive myself for going completely off the deep end. But forgiveness was not my primary concern at the moment, so why offer such leverage to the abstract?

What if he comes home and finds me rifling through his underwear drawer? Not that I would rifle, but for argument's sake, what if I did? What if he had just stepped out for a moment to pick up the blonde bimbo and bring her back for a roll in the hay?

And what if?

What if?

What if?

And what if again?

I could not live by *what if*; I had to live by *what is*, and the door *was* open and the only thing separating me from his world was a conscience that only worked on a part-time basis these days.

So what if I closed the door and called it a day? But then again, what if I didn't? In the lap of despair, I made my final decision. I slid through the opening and went inside. Sometimes we do things, even wrong things, just because it's been so long since we've done the *right* thing that to do another *wrong* thing doesn't add or take away from that which we have become.

Another day of humiliation and degradation, embarrassment and heartbreak wasn't really that big of a deal to me. I had already lost so much, destroyed so much, denied so much, and shamed myself to the point where I had nothing left. And I had *nothing* to lose—or so I believed. But I was about to find out how truly wrong I was. There's always something to lose, even for the man who has nothing.

Entering through the patio poured me out into his kitchen. I took note of every element around me: a blender that appeared tilted from a distance. Toasted bread crumbs on floors and counters. Poorly wrapped bread drying from the overexposure to air.

A trash can impregnated by giant cereal boxes and a water cooler emptied of its sustenance. Oh, and his scent. The exfoliation of his odor was groping me everywhere.

I shouldn't be here.

It felt wrong.

I hung my head for a minute and grieved and mourned and dropped a tear or two, disappointed in the woman I had become.

It was so easy to get caught up and then before you know it, carried away. It was effortless to obsess without realizing what obsession was because I wanted it so bad. Because I would do anything and I would say anything and I would give anything, including my dignity, the most proud possession I owned, in order to obtain it. I would have sold my soul to the devil if he could have guaranteed that I wouldn't die alone.

If the devil could guarantee it, I would have him put it in writing and even if the terms of the document stated that I would eventually end up in hell, *still* I would have signed. And I would have justified that it couldn't be any worse than the hell I was already in. If for one moment of earthly existence I could have authentically experienced unrequited love, I would have declared, "Devil, where in the hell do I sign?"

I had given my consent to the devil without acknowledgment of the fact. And *this* is what I had become.

And for what?

And for whom?

And why?

Was my life so bad or disappointing, boring, lonely, tired, or sad the day I met Eddie, that I easily shed my skin and stepped into his and begged him to do the same, only to take a turn for the worse when that didn't happen?

I wanted to cry so bad that it took all of my strength to keep my composure. I stared at the garbage can for a long time because I wanted to dive in head first and disappear with my checkered past.

Michael Morgan, the man doesn't love you.

Nor does he want to be with you.

Nor is he responding.

You have shed many tears on behalf of someone who could not shed them back.

You have chased and hunted and tortured yourself for something that wasn't real. Indeed, you shared a moment with him, but how much more obvious should it be that the moment *has* passed. And the only thing that keeps you connected to this man is your *imagination*.

Lucidity in the eleventh hour brought me back to myself. Clarity was staring me in the face delivering perplexity in question form: *What are you going to do about it? What are you going to do?* I had planned to turn around and walk out of his life for good . . .

But my thoughts were hollowed by moans.

Moans that startled me, rendering me motionless like cement.

I didn't move.

Didn't swallow.

Didn't breathe.

I didn't think that anyone was here but me.

I didn't want to listen, but they were growing more intense, the moans. They were brisk, hurried, violent, and raging. Were they sexual in nature? I didn't know. Enticement pulled me in the direction of the sound, much like the moon pulls on the tide.

I knew that moan.

I recognized it.

I eased down the hall like a ghost walking on water. I was being called toward the stage to play out the scene that would ultimately label this play a tragedy.

I stood in a trance just outside the bedroom with eyes fixated on the door, slightly cracked. It wasn't a large crack. It was just enough to allow a single beam of light slight entrance. The door's gap was wide enough to insert a sliver of hair or a thin dream through. It was just enough to bend me toward temptation, prompting me to lay one finger against the heavy structure and push. I didn't push a lot. I barely pushed a little and the door gently opened.

And my eyes did a wild dance.

And my blood pressure exploded.

And my respiration became labored.

And my aneurysm cashed in on its payday.

And I couldn't believe what I saw.

And I saw what I couldn't believe.

And my vision went black.

And the room turned white.

And my heart blew up.

And my soul quickly followed.

And I died standing up.

And I died standing there.

And in the end I finally let out a giant SCREAM!

And as the echo of my screams bounced against walls, they quickly untangled themselves from one another. He was on top. She was on the bottom, It was Molly Wood and Eddie, but tonight his name was John, and Molly was back on the block now, acting out her childhood fantasies of being a prostitute.

You?

You and my best friend?

My soul mate has just disintegrated to ash.

Oh, my God, I thought I'd die.

And die.

And die.

Or better yet, kill them both so that we could all feel better about the whole damn thing. Insanity had risen to an all-time high, laughing out loud and at itself for sport.

It cried out.

Fell down.

Released itself and ran free, all in the name of liberation and the prostitution of oneself for cash. *Molly Wood, I would have given you a loan if you needed cash that bad.* And even though I was unemployed and money didn't come that easy, I would have stolen from my own mother's house to keep her off my man— and that's when I knew that I was sick.

And hurt.

And my hurt turned to hate.

And that hate turned to blood.

This was my story? Whose story? A blue story and sadder yet, a true story of a black woman who loved a white man too much. And in the end, he poured savvy gravy all over me. And it stuck to my flesh and burned off my skin. And now that it's all said and done and no one can stand to look at anyone anymore, where the hell do we go from here?

No one said a word and we all became convenient deaf-mutes to a lethal situation. And I began to wonder if they even knew. I bet they didn't even remember that we had all known each other once upon a time when a white mime fell for a black girl in the back of a seedy bar while her junkie friend gave free fucks in a bathroom stall in exchange for tequila shots.

Damn that was deep.

Molly shrunk into the bathroom and shut the door.

Quittin' time.

Eddie sat down on the edge of the bed, fumbling to cover his nakedness as if I had not seen it all before.

And I . . .

What was left of me?

Broken.

Bruised.

Battered.

Blown up.

And blown away . . .

Too zombied to respond.

CRAVE

Too hurt to cry out.

Too defeated to try and win.

Too angry to throw a punch.

Too rageful to pull a gun.

Too devastated to die again . . .

I turned my back on them both, walked out, and disappeared.

27

HURTIN' HEALIN', AND POETRY

When Mother opened the door, I collapsed into her arms and wailed, bumrushing the barriers of our "polite" relationship. And this only put her on full tactical alert. She was prepared to defend whatever needed protecting and equipped to fix whatever had been broken.

She was willing to rebuild all that had been destroyed because that's what mommies do best, even the crazy ones. *Sorry Mother, a little too late, but I love you incessantly for trying.* She could not comprehend my hysteria, and it would take some time before she understood what had actually happened. In the interim, she scanned my body with her eyes searching for damage and blood.

Mother, my wounds are of an internal nature, and you shall find no spoil on my clothing or flesh. Through my muffled sobs and outbursts of emotion, eventually she would stack the words on top of one another to build a story.

This story.

It was a love story built one word at a time, lopsided on the heavy end of crave. And standing here in this spot in my mother's living room, I saw so many flashbacks of a childhood that should have been better than it was.

I saw a cantankerous mother who had beaten her husband down with words and neediness. And she still didn't know it to this day. I saw my papa, a once decent man who just couldn't take it anymore. And then I saw me—a child who felt abandoned by her father twice, once while living and once while dead. I also saw a mother who was too consumed by her own pain to comfort her traumatized child who had lost a father twice. I saw this little girl stuff her grief into her back pocket because it was "inconvenient" and rude to expose it to her fragile mother.

This was the same little girl who had grown into a woman and fallen for the *first* man who appeared to love her. For the first man who wanted to teach her to ride a bike the right way and not just push her into a tree because it was easier than actually taking the time to instruct her properly. For the first man aside from her papa to read her bedtime stories—Goldilocks, her favorite.

No wonder I couldn't breathe without him. Eddie was the first man who came into my world on the tail end of the way my papa had left it. How could I *not* hold on?

"Do you know what it feels like to be me?" I asked my mother, looking dead into her eyes, holding her accountable. Not for all of my wounds, just for the *deep* ones.

"You okay?" she mumbled.

"Do you know what it feels like to be me?" I asked again.

"No," she said flatly. "No, I don't."

"Do you know why you don't know?" I posed the question. She didn't answer, just backed away.

"Because my whole life your only concern was what it felt like to be *you*," I said quietly as I walked away. "I miss Papa so much," I said before entering my childhood bedroom and shutting the door.

"I know," I heard her say from the other side of the door. And I was quite surprised by this acknowledgment.

I curled up into my bed and fell asleep.

I was awakened later that night by my mother, who was standing at the foot of the bed. For a moment I thought I saw her clutching a steak knife against her bosom, preparing to chop me to bits and pieces for speaking my mind, but it was an illusion.

"I could have done better," she said teary and regretful. "But I did the *best* I could."

I didn't know what to say. This was the moment I had waited for my whole life—a *real* conversation with the Hollywood starlet wannabe, where she actually acknowledged that not every movie has a happy ending and we don't all get to ride off into the sunset.

"It wasn't easy for me after your father died," she said emotionally.

"For either of us," I added, to make sure she didn't get carried away on the hurricane of her own emotion.

"You know, Michael," she said, "you have so many reasons to crucify me for the job I did as your mother. But I guess I just always hoped that you wouldn't."

And just like that she left, leaving me no room to respond or to feel.

Damn.

She was still fragile, and I was just too decent to betray her fragility. She hoped that I wouldn't crucify her, and I had obliged. Although on some level I did resent her, because there is nothing more valuable or irreplaceable than a mother's love. And a mother who authentically comes outside of herself enough to love her child can make the difference between that child getting her validation from within or spending an entire lifetime searching for it from others.

I looked around my bedroom, and fortunately it hadn't changed much since the eighth grade. I still had Michael Jackson posters on the wall and Chaka Khan LPs on the nightstand. *Thank you, Mother, for not throwing away the little girl I used to be.* I could at the very least thank her for that.

I crawled into bed and rolled into a ball and sobbed. What had become of my life? The loss of my father and the sting of Eddie penetrated me to the bone.

I grieved for the truth, slowly watching it unfold like a heating croissant. I chased its patterns and twists, struggling to understand its intricate layout. I connected the dots, creating my own definition of reality. It wasn't difficult to see the truth, because the truth was hell-bent on being seen. It had gripped a blunt object, cracked me upside the head, and taunted, "Can you see me now, girl? Can you see me?"

Oh, I see you, I acknowledged with eyes of understanding. *And what do I do with you now that I see you?*

What would become of my friendship with Molly?

And what of my obsession for Eddie?

I slid from the bed and onto my knees for a closing conversation with Jesus. I didn't want Jesus to get the wrong idea and think I was desperate or something, but *I was desperate or something*. And on my knees I offered the most powerful prayer I knew.

It contained no words.

No thoughts.

No requests.

No promises.

No unrealistic expectations.

No magic.

No dramatics.

No drama.

No stage.

No dream.

No begging.

Just tears.

I wrote Molly Wood off that night. It wasn't easy to do, but it was necessary to move on with my life. My mother always said Molly and I were from two different worlds, and at long last I concurred. And the common ground we shared once upon a time did not seem so "common" anymore.

Though I knew her encounter with Eddie was "business" and not a malicious intent to harm me, I also came to realize that Molly was in the business of breaking hearts. And for every John she slept with, there was "someone on the other end" who loved them. And with regard to the search for my prince, I offered my final prayer to God in the form of poetry:

Good night, sweet prince. I shall weep at your departure. I have searched for you all of my life. I have checked under subway benches and bus stops. I have played peekaboo against abandoned buildings waiting to catch a glimpse of your shadow. I've jumped inside barren trenches and gone underground on the slight chance you might be sharing living quarters with the groundhog.

I have climbed rooftops, scaled high-rises. I have simmered in seedy clubs and bathed in bad associations because I truly believed you were there—I just thought you were scared and hiding.

I have jeopardized myself chasing trains that I thought you had boarded. I've grabbed the tail end of planes, fearing you may have landed and taken off before you found me. I have traveled the globe in hopes I would recognize your face and then I have gone back again fearful I missed you the first time around.

I have peered through eyeglasses, looking glasses, and magnifying glasses searching for your footprints, and have even enlisted the help of psychics to convince me you exist.

I have gazed into the eyes of other women's husbands and boyfriends wondering, "Could it be you?" And wondered if you'd missed me altogether by accident.

I have traced steps on cemetery grounds on morbid days believing you had already come, gone, and would never come again and that perhaps that was the real reason for your no-show status.

I've stolen peeks through picture windows at dinnertime staring at the back of his head, and his head, begging you to just turn around.

I have pulled double duty at bridal showers and weddings, standing up for her and standing in for the other. I have watched everyone I know celebrate the arrival of her prince, everyone but me.

Good night, sweet prince, I shall weep at your departure. If you came, I didn't see you. If you spoke, I didn't hear you. If you were real, I didn't feel you. And if you loved me once upon a time, I guess I didn't love you back the same.

Good night, sweet prince.

Good night.

It's time for me to move on with my life and experience a new day.

A real day.

My first day

Without crave.

Amen.

28

A DAY WITHOUT CRAVE

Time didn't close the wounds completely, but it did stitch them up quite nicely. My heart slowly resumed normal activity with beats and rhythm. It had been several weeks since my immersion into savvy gravy, and the burns were scabbed and protected. My extremities gave way to movement and I could feel myself again. My tear ducts were *almost* empty, but my heart was still very tender. I avoided vulnerable situations and climates that bred sensitivity.

I found solace with my mother and we came to our own understanding of peace, whatever that was. I came to know her in new and different ways, more as a person, less as a mother. And this gave me more latitude to see her as *human*. After much deliberation, I finally accepted a job in Denver, which was two hours from Shilo, to work as a beautician for a well-known mortuary.

Amazing.

The world looks different when you view it from your feet instead of seeing it from the ground on your knees. I had survived desperation's darkest hour and managed to walk through the black hole all the while reminding myself to just keep breathing.

I found the guts to walk through the fire and embrace the flame. I was finally able to grieve the loss of my father. I eased into the discomfort that sustaining such a loss brings—the loneliness, the neediness. I tapped into the reservoirs of my strength, courage, and wisdom.

I took a temporary break from men. I didn't hunt them down, nor did I allow myself to become easy prey. Instead, I spent the days enjoying my own company and that of my mother.

I reacquainted myself with the women my mother had once upon a time insisted I have a relationship with: Alice Walker, Audre Lourde, Gwendolyn Brooks, Sonia Sanchez. And I fell in love with all of them, but each for different reasons. I dove into the creative aspects of my persona, and to my surprise, discovered a budding writer crouching in a little, dark corner.

I found that when I didn't consume myself with questions, life kindly granted me the answers. When I didn't strain so hard to see, the picture automatically came into focus. When I learned the art of sitting still, I could finally feel all that I had been missing by living life on fast forward.

I learned to appreciate the little things, like the way a bird builds its nest, or the way an ant organizes its journey. I learned to hum instead of sing and bend instead of lean. I learned that harmony was simply the process of blending the sane voices with insane ones.

I washed my face.

I restyled my hair.

I cleaned up my act.

And soon the day came when I left my childhood bedroom for the last time, kissed my mother good-bye, and reentered the world of a grown-up. But before I did, there was one more stop to make.

No chicken wings.

No potato salad or booze.

No toothpicks, tampons, or batteries.

No lighter fluid, charcoal, or canned sardines.

No quick fix, no attitude, and most of all, no exceptions.

In other words, I knocked on Mabel's door empty-handed. She opened it with her usual suspicious eye cast downward upon me, but I didn't care. She didn't scare me anymore, not even with those devil-red eyes. I knew Mabel had a gift, and like so many gifted people, she was seen as "disturbed."

"I just came to say good-bye," I said.

"Oh," she said nodding. "You must have seen the future with your own eyes for a change."

"Yeah, something like that," I said. "You take care of yourself, Mabel."

"What do you care what I take?" she snapped, consistent with her nature. I couldn't help but chuckle, because Mabel was a brute and she probably would always be one, but that was also part of her charm.

The key to understanding Mabel was accepting her as she was. I started down the steps and she called after my shadow, which had all but disappeared into the concrete.

"I'm sorry things did not work out the way your heart had wished them to be," she said. Her words set me back a beat, not much, but enough to stir tears. I couldn't see Mabel from where I stood, but that didn't stop me from a sarcastic "Thanks," whispered under my breath. And though I barely said it, I think she heard me and hobbled to the edge of the steps, which surprised me, because she never came outside. She held onto the railing with one hand and the rickety cane with the other.

"Michael, I do have the gift of sight. That much is true, but there is a heavy responsibility that comes with it," she said.

"Really?" I asked, somewhat curious.

"Those who see the future are under grave obligation *not* to disturb it," she said. And this declaration staggered me.

"Mabel," I had to ask, "if you can't *do* anything about it, then what makes it so great that you can see it?"

"Exactly," she said with a peculiar smile. "Now you know why I am always so cranky," she said, before hobbling back to her apartment and slamming the door.

I had not been home in a few weeks because I had been staying with my mother. When I opened the door to my apartment the place looked exactly the same as I had left it. Perhaps there *were* things time chose not to disturb after all. The bedspread still wore the same wrinkle left in it the day it was made in a hurry.

A coffee mug on the counter bore the same ring around the center with the same Lancôme lipstick stain on the outer edge. The tantalizing color Jezebel held up well under duress, I might add. My stockings still hung from the shower door, obviously dry by now. My hair gel evaporated because I left the top off. My toothbrush bristles dried out and turned rock hard.

My Sade CD, *Lover's Rock,* was still in the CD player, and I couldn't resist playing "The King of Sorrow." I sat back on my oversized couch and buried my head against the backdrop as the cooing songbird summed up my existence. Her blend of eroticism and sadness brought devastation to the surface. It brought it up easy and delivered it to me hard. It soothed me in the beginning, rocked me in the middle, held me steady for the duration, and by the end of the song, it had taken to task the chore of strangling me to death. Warm tears brought little to no comfort as my head moved up and down, consistently but with a strong groove as I sang backup for Sade without shame.

The scene built the bridge connecting me to the past, drifting me back to the days of Lorenzo and Antonio. I still feel you. *Still feel you.* Michael, Stuart, Damian, Diego, Marcus, and Troy, I still feel you. *Still feel you.* I descended into the moment of all that could have been imagining the faint scent of Eddie's cologne, Sky's scent, their drama, my pain. Each memory delivered a splintered prick of pain. Every time I closed my eyes, I was forced to greet the ghost of another man that got away. My apartment contained so much history that I knew it would be impossible for me to stay.

When the words "Time to blow this Popsicle stand" echoed

through my apartment, I trembled in my skin. And when I saw that it was Molly Wood who was poking her head through my doorway, a surge of emotion swelled within. Dear reader: Beware of those who come bearing the gift of friendship and leave with your sex partner without your consent.

"What are you doing here?" I demanded sharply. And of course she pretended to be deaf, so I asked again, "What are you doing here?"

"I miss you, honey bunny," was all she could say, inviting herself inside. I shook my head, turned my back, and walked toward the bedroom.

"I'm moving, Molly," I said irritably. "I don't have to time to chat."

"Where you going, honey bunny?" she asked on my heels with urgency.

I pulled a large suitcase from the closet and began filling it with clothes. I didn't bother to answer her question because she didn't need to know. As she watched me pack, she shifted back and forth nervously.

"What about all of your stuff?"

"I'll be back for it."

"So where you going?" she asked again.

Silence.

"Michael, I didn't know he was the guy . . ." she started, then stopped. Her blissful ignorance pulled my chain even harder. "How was I supposed to know?"

"All in a day's work, right, Molly?" I snapped, throwing my undergarments in the suitcase.

"That's not fair!" she said. "The guy was just looking to get off. There's no emotional attachment with it!"

"So that's supposed to make me feel better about you fucking him?"

"It was just sex!" she defended. "Sex. Not love. Sex!"

"So nice of you to differentiate between the two," I said in disbelief, shaking my head again. "You must be real proud of yourself, Molly."

"Look, honey bunny," she said trying to sound sincere. "I been coming over here every day for two weeks looking for you so I could tell you I'm sorry."

"I'm not your honey bunny," I snapped.

"Michael, tell me we'll get through this shit and still be friends. You're the only real friend I've ever had." I softened a bit as I reflected on our history together, a history that always commanded much more than I could give.

"It was just business . . . you know," she reaffirmed. "It wasn't personal . . . it's not like I had an orgasm or anything."

"Molly," I said grabbing my bags. "There are some things in life you never get over."

"I know, baby, but we can get through this—"

"This," I interrupted, "is one of those things," I concluded before escorting her out of my home and locking the door behind us.

She was in tears, almost hysterics, begging and pleading as I walked toward my car.

"Michael!" screamed Molly. "Michael!"

I just kept walking.

"You're my best friend. My *best* friend in the whole wide world!" she screamed. "You're my very *best* friend! My *best* friend!"

I didn't look back but found myself giving way to emotion as tears streamed down my cheeks. It wasn't easy to walk away, but it was so damn necessary. There would be no time, no room or reason to ever look back again. Sometimes we outgrow the places in our lives and sometimes we outgrow the people. And on rare occasions, we even outgrow both.

I got in my car, closed the door, and rolled up the windows to drown out the sound of desperation. As I drove away, I caught a final glimpse of Molly Wood in my rearview mirror, jumping up and down in the street, waiving her arms in the air, mouthing my name. A lifetime of friendship circled the drain and went down *easy*.

I would probably miss her someday, but not today. And that made it possible for me to move on without second and third glances. I didn't say it made it easy, just *possible*.

And as I blazed down the road to freedom, I got to the street where Eddie lived. I slowed down, then stopped and turned off the engine.

I could have died right there, but I didn't, because I was bigger than that. And because I was brighter and stronger than that. And because I finally accepted that my papa was gone and I could not reincarnate him through Eddie or any other man for that matter. I had made the long painful journey home to myself and I was not about to give up on me again.

I stopped at the end of his street, but I did not turn my

wheels in the direction of his house. For there was no need to crawl to his front door and demand that he love me. I had begun to love myself. And somewhere between here and there, something snapped and crave began to die its own death.

I smiled.

I laughed out loud.

And I cried a tear or two.

Then I restarted my engine and hightailed it to the freeway, where the big green sign promised Denver in about 122 miles.

Like I said a long, long time ago: Everything in the dark eventually does a slow crawl to the light. Every symphony must be played even if it falls upon deaf ears. Every poet must pursue his own verse and every writer must make love to the world he has chosen to create. And with all truths foregoing, every fish must find its own true pond to swim in. It was time to finally go and find my pond.

For there are some destinies that cannot be fulfilled, like the friendship between Molly Wood and me. And then there are others that simply disappear, like that of mine and Eddie's. And only God, Mabel, and time know why.

As I sped down the highway, I knew I would never see Sky, Eddie, or Molly again. But I also knew that eventually my life would transcend it all. And just for the hell of it, when it did, I might actually sit down, gather my thoughts, write a book, and call it *Crave*.

READING GROUP GUIDE

CRAVE

1. How would you categorize the relationship between Michael and her mother? Michael and her father? Would you classify them as a dysfunctional family? Explain.

2. Emotionally, did Michael need more than her parents could realistically provide? Would you classify her as a needy child?

3. What role did Mabel, the chicken-wing eating psychic, represent in Michael's life? Do you believe that Mabel truly had a gift to foresee the future?

4. Describe the relationship between Michael and Eddie. Why did Michael become so attached to this particular man? Do you feel that Eddie encouraged Michael's obsession? Explain.

5. What was the nature of Michael's relationship with Sky? Was sleeping with him a mistake? Why or why not?

6. What do you think brought Michael and Molly together? What do you think tore them apart?

7. Is Michael's story a representation of some of the basic challenges we all face in the pursuit of love? Explain.

8. If you had been a character in the novel, what advice would you have given to Michael regarding her situation with Eddie?

9. Have you experienced a craving in your own life? Explain.

For more reading group suggestions visit
www.stmartins.com

Get a
Griffin 🦅 St. Martin's Griffin